Collection
The Magician

More adventures of

Littlenose

Littlenose Collection: The Explorer

Littlenose
Collection
The Magician

John Grant   Illustrated by **Ross Collins**

SIMON AND SCHUSTER

The collection first published in Great Britain in 2014 by Simon and Schuster UK Ltd
A CBS COMPANY

Two-Eyes' Friends was first published in 1969
Littlenose the Hunter was first published in 1972
Littlenose the Fisherman was first published in 1974
Littlenose the Magician was first published in 1975
Two-Eyes' Revenge, Littlenose's Holiday and Bigfoot were first published in 1976
The Old Man's Spear and Squeaky were first published in 1977
Littlenose's Cousins was first published in 1979
Littlenose the Joker and The Fox Fur Robe were first published in 1983
Littlenose and Two-Eyes, The Amber Pendant and Roch-a-Bye Littlenose
were first published in 1986
in Great Britain by The British Broadcasting Corporation

1 3 5 7 9 10 8 6 4 2

Simon & Schuster UK Ltd
1st Floor, 222 Gray's Inn Road
London
WC1X 8HB

Simon & Schuster Australia, Sydney
Simon & Schuster India, New Delhi

A CIP catalogue record for this book
is available from the British Library.

ISBN 978-1-47112-137-1
eBook 978-1-47112-138-8

Printed and bound by CPI Group (UK) Ltd, Croydon, CR0 4YY

www.simonandschuster.co.uk
www.simonandschuster.com.au

Contents

Littlenose
the Magician

JOHN GRANT

Illustrations by ROSS COLLINS

Contents

Littlenose the Magician

In the days when Littlenose lived, the most
important person in the tribe was the Old
Man. But, only a little less important was
the Doctor. He looked after the sick, as
you might expect, but he had other
important duties as well.

For instance, he foretold the future.
This he did by watching pictures in the
fire, or by observing the flight of birds.

But his favourite method was to take out a pack of white birch bark squares with strange markings on them. He spread them out on a flat rock, then turned them up one at a time, muttering as he did so. The people would crowd round his cave saying: "He is going to make a prediction." Then a meeting would be called later in the day at which the Doctor would raise his arms and pronounce in a solemn voice something like: "There is going to be a hard winter!" And considering this was the Ice Age, he had never been wrong!

Littlenose didn't think much of either the Doctor's nasty-tasting medicines or his fortunetelling, but he was filled with awe at the Doctor's other job, that of Tribal Magician. He had only the vaguest idea what magic was, and he had never seen the

Doctor actually perform any, but he heard a lot about it. He knew, for instance, that he could make a coloured pebble vanish and produce it from someone's ear; he had heard that, with the right magic words, a handful of old bones could become a bouquet of flowers; and there was the story of a rabbit which the doctor had produced from an empty fur hood.

Someone had once asked why he didn't use his magic to help in useful things like hunting and rain-making as the Straightnoses did. The Doctor was horrified. "It's not for us to meddle with the powers of darkness," he said warningly. "Look what it's done for the Straightnoses. You wouldn't want to end up like them, would you?" And as that was the last thing anyone wanted, it was never mentioned again.

There had been a lot of talk lately about the Doctor and magic, but Littlenose was more concerned with the preparations for the Sun Dance. This was the great mid-winter festival, like a huge party, with singing and dancing and feasting. Presents were given, and everyone had a marvellous time far into the night, even past bed-time for grownups. This year there was to be an extra treat. Occasionally, the Doctor had been persuaded to give a demonstration of magic as part of the entertainment. His last appearance had been before Littlenose was old enough to attend the Sun Dance. In the few days left, the Doctor was very busy, and was quite huffy if anyone arrived at his cave with a sore stomach or toothache. All they got were some dried herbs or a quick drink of something discouraging from the Doctor's wife.

She was his assistant and nurse, and she spent most of her time out of sight at home. Littlenose thought that she was probably ashamed of being so ugly. She was tall and skinny, by Neanderthal standards, with a nose not much bigger than Littlenose's own. She might have been called Littlenose too, but her hair was long, straight and yellow, so she was called Goldie.

It was rumoured that she came from a distant tribe and it was she who had taught the Doctor all he knew.

The Sun Dance came at last and, as usual, it was even better than Littlenose remembered. When they had danced and sung themselves hoarse, and even Littlenose had eaten himself to a standstill, the Old Man stepped forward and announced: "And now, for your delight and delectation, a fabulous feast of mystery and merriment proudly presented by the great. . .DOCTOR!"

The doctor swept into the circle with a flourish. He wore a cloak of some smooth, black fur, and a hood over his head. The hood covered his face so that his eyes shone out from a pair of holes. He looked mysterious and rather frightening. As the applause began to die away, the Old Man threw out an arm and shouted, "Assisted by the glamorous Goldie!"

The glamorous Goldie ran on to even louder applause. She wore two rabbit ears in her hair, while the rest consisted of all that was left of the rabbit . . . including the tail.

The magic show was everything Littlenose expected and more. Coloured pebbles appeared and reappeared. Old bones became bunches of flowers and, not one but two rabbits were pulled mysteriously from a fur hood. The audience cheered and clapped while Littlenose's eyes grew wider and wider at the wonder of it all. Then the Doctor and the glamorous Goldie carried forward what looked like the trunk of a tree. But as they set it up in front of the audience, Littlenose saw that the log had been hollowed out so that it was really only a shell of very thin wood and bark. As it was laid on the ground, he could also see that it had been split down the centre with the top half forming a sort of lid.

The Doctor held up his hand for silence. "I shall now attempt, with the assistance of the glamorous Goldie, one of the most hazardous feats of magic known. I must ask for complete silence. Thank you."

With a flourish, he lifted the lid of the hollow log and held the glamorous Goldie by the hand while she climbed inside. She smiled prettily, waved, and lay down so that her head stuck out at one end and her feet at the other. The Doctor stooped down and picked up the biggest axe Littlenose had ever seen. The audience gasped as the Doctor swung it up without effort, and held their breath as he stood in the circle of torchlight, which sparkled along the axe's sharp edge. Then, with a crash, the axe hurtled down on to the tree trunk and the glamorous Goldie!

Splinters flew in all directions as the blade buried itself in the ground. People screamed. Some fainted. Littlenose felt sick. But the Doctor was not finished yet. He quickly removed the axe and pulled the two halves of the log apart. There was a clear gap where the glamorous Goldie's middle should have been. Which wasn't surprising . . . and hardly magic!

What was surprising, and could only be magic, was her nodding head and smiling face sticking out of one half, and her wriggling toes sticking out of the other. The audience was again silent as the Doctor quickly pushed the halves together. He waved

his arm, shouted a magic word and raised the lid. The glamorous Goldie stood up and waved. There wasn't a mark on her. She bowed to the audience, and Littlenose expected her top half to fall off. But it didn't, and the Doctor and the glamorous Goldie went off to thunderous applause.

In the weeks following the Sun Dance, Littlenose could think of nothing else but magic. He even tried some, but without success. Things just refused to disappear, and Dad almost split his sides laughing as Littlenose frantically waved an old bone in the air, trying to turn it into a bunch of flowers. "Come on, Littlenose," he said, "you must do better than that. How about cutting a lady in half? I'm sure Mum would help. That is, if you could get her inside a hollow log. Ha! Ha! Ha!" Mum said, "That's not funny."

"Just you wait," said Littlenose. "When I've learned to do a piece of magic, you'll get the biggest surprise of your lives!"

After a few days, Littlenose decided that his magic was getting nowhere. But he had an idea. He would find out how the Doctor did his. He couldn't very well ask him straight out, but if he could creep close enough to his cave, he might see him at work. It was risky. He had once heard the story of a boy who had tried just this and had been turned into a frog!

Next morning, Littlenose set off for the Doctor's cave. As he approached, he could hear voices from inside. He tip-toed to the entrance. The Doctor and his wife were seated with their backs to him, busy at some task . . . probably more magic. Littlenose edged closer but, whatever their task was, they were keeping it well hidden from intruders. He was about to leave, when something caught his attention.

Lying on a rocky ledge just inside the cave entrance was a stick, thick as a finger and about half the length of Littlenose's arm.
It was stained with strange patterns and Littlenose remembered that he had last

seen it at the Sun Dance, when the Doctor had used it to wave or point at things he wanted to change into something else or to disappear. In a moment, Littlenose had made up his mind. He would borrow the stick. He wouldn't ask for the loan of it. Just borrow it. In a flash the stick was under his hunting robe. Then Littlenose hurried home as fast as he could.

Slipping to the back of the cave, he tried out the magic stick. He waved it, tapped it and shook it, but nothing disappeared. And nothing changed into anything else. But Littlenose wasn't downhearted. "Practice," he said to himself. "That's what I need." But before he could get any practice, he heard Dad calling him.

"A herd of bison has been seen nearby," said Dad, "and we're going out with a party to hunt them. Get your things. We're leaving immediately."

Littlenose put on his hunting robe and picked up his boy-size spear. He wondered about the magic stick for a moment, then decided to bind it along the shaft of the spear. This made it easy to carry and was unlikely to be noticed.

The hunters had barely left the caves before they realised that something odd was happening. The air was strangely mild and there was a slight thaw, very unusual for this time of year. They trudged on through the wood, Littlenose and Two-Eyes bringing up the rear of the column. They stopped to rest for a moment and Littlenose whispered to Two-Eyes, "Look, there's a robin," and pointed up into a tree. And at that second a great lump of melting snow slid from the tree and fell on one of the hunters with a thump. The man struggled to his feet and shook his fist at Littlenose. "That you up to your tricks?" he shouted. "Throwing things?"

"I didn't throw anything," said Littlenose. "I just pointed. Like that." He did it just as a pine branch, weakened by the weight of snow it was carrying, snapped with a loud crack and tumbled to the ground. The hunters all looked at Littlenose. They looked at the spear he was still pointing. He looked at the stick tied to the spear and began to wonder. However, after a bit of muttering among themselves, the hunters went on their way, but kept a watchful eye on Littlenose.

At length, they reached a small valley with a frozen stream at the bottom. Nosey, the chief stalker, was warily inching his way across but he didn't feel at all safe. Littlenose stood with Two-Eyes some way back from the stream and watched. "I think you're too heavy to cross there, Two-Eyes," he said, and pointed with his spear. There was a loud crack, then a wild yell from Nosey as the ice broke under him and he

vanished into the freezing water.
Littlenose dropped the spear as if it were
red hot.

While the hunters hauled a shivering
Nosey on to the bank, Littlenose untied
the stick and wondered what to do with it.
He had a feeling that just throwing it away
would be no good. He should never have
taken it without asking. He tucked it out of
sight in his furs and planned to give it back
to its rightful owner just as soon as he

reached home. And it looked as if that would be sooner than he'd expected. The bison had gone, leaving no trace, and Nosey was sneezing and shivering from his ducking.

The hunters decided to stop for the night and made a rough shelter out of tree branches and hunting robes. The air had turned heavy and clammy, while inky, black clouds began to pile up in the sky. They had a cold supper and, while there was still some light left, Littlenose wandered off for a stroll before turning in. He carried the magic stick under his robe and had decided to try once more to make it work for him. After all, the disasters of earlier in the day could have been chance. Perhaps.

When he was out of sight of the camp, he picked up a handful of twigs and waved the stick over them. They were meant to turn into a bunch of flowers. Nothing happened, except that a large spot of rain fell on his nose. And that wasn't magic. He tried it on pebbles but they remained obstinately unchanged. He even tapped himself on the head, and was relieved that he didn't turn into a frog. He gave up. The rain was beginning to fall heavily now and the snow grew wet and mushy under his feet.

Littlenose shouted angrily at the stick and shook it hard. "Call yourself magic? You're just an old bit of firewood. I dare you to do something magic!"

There was a blinding flash and a deafening bang. A solitary pine tree high on the hill in front of him was split from top to bottom by a jagged bolt of lightning.

Littlenose fell to the ground in terror and watched the smouldering remains of the tree, as the rain poured down about him and the thunder crashed and boomed about the sky.

Littlenose lay awake all night, quaking with terror. Dad and the other hunters were not sympathetic. "Fancy a big boy like you afraid of thunder," they laughed.

As soon as the hunting party reached home, Littlenose lost no time in returning the stick. He tried to sneak it back the way he had got it but, just as he was creeping up to the cave entrance, a voice said: "What do you think you're playing at?" it was the Doctor.

Littlenose was trapped. "This is it," he thought. "I'll be a frog any minute."

He stood up and held out the stick.

"I was bringing this back. You see, it's like this. I was —"

But the Doctor cut him short. "Oh thanks. Didn't know I'd dropped it. Didn't really matter." And he casually broke the stick into pieces and threw them in the fire.

Littlenose was aghast. The Doctor spoke again. "Here's something for your trouble." And he tossed a coloured pebble at Littlenose. He caught it . . . and it was an apple! "Now, off you go and don't bother me, Sonny. I've got a lot to do."

"Thank you," said Littlenose, thoroughly perplexed. He looked at the apple. Was it magic? He suddenly didn't care about magic any more. He knew he managed to get into enough trouble without the aid of magic.

He started to run towards the cave, shouting, "Come on, Two-Eyes. I've got an apple. You can have half."

The Old Man's Spear

The Old Man was leader of the tribe
because he was not only the oldest
member but the wisest. No one knew how
old he was, and they had even less idea of
the extent of his wisdom. As a young man
he had been handsome, strong, swift,
and a famous hunter. But now he was bald,
fat and a bit short of wind. It was years
since he last hunted but he didn't need to,

as he was given a share of all the tribe's food. The Old Man's job was to organise everyone else; and he did it very well.

Yet one spring day when the sun shone, the trees were beginning to turn green and the snow had vanished, the Old Man summoned the hunters to a meeting.

Dad and Littlenose (he was an apprentice hunter), hurried along wondering what calamity was about to strike this time. For the Old Man's meetings usually spelled trouble. When they were all assembled, the Old Man climbed onto a boulder and addressed them. "I intend," he said, "to go hunting. I want you to arrange everything. Make it a week today. Any questions? No? That's it, then. Thank you." And he turned away into his cave.

The hunters were astonished and there was a lot of muttering as the meeting broke up. "Hunting! At his age! He's daft!"

Dad said much the same thing. "You can't say things like that," said Mum, aghast. "He is, after all, the Leader!"

Littlenose saw nothing odd in the Old Man's wanting a bit of fun. He thought it must be very dull with nothing to do all day but make speeches, study the Time Sticks, and tell people what to do. And although Dad and the rest of the grown-up hunters still thought the whole idea ridiculous, the other members of the tribe began to think like Littlenose. They got more and more enthusiastic until, instead of the hunters planning an official hunt for the Old Man, it had become a grand day out and picnic for the whole tribe. Of course, there would still be some hunting, because that, after all, was what the Old Man wanted.

The day of the Old Man's hunt came at last. And there had never been a hunt like it. The hunters hoped that there would never be one like it again. The hunting party, if that's what you could call it, assembled in front of the caves soon after breakfast. Everyone was there. Men, women, children, old people bobbling along on sticks and babies in arms. Dad, Nosey and other men shouted themselves hoarse trying to get some sort of order, while babies cried and older children chased one another through the crowd. When the Old Man at last appeared everyone cheered. He carried a spear that looked even older than himself. "Well, what are we waiting for?" he said. "Let's go."

An ordinary hunting party would consist

of no more than a dozen men, carrying spears and a few pieces of gear for camping out. They would march in a straight line behind the tracker and be absolutely silent, for fear that they would scare away the animals they were hunting. But this was a whole tribe! They carried babies and baskets of food. And they straggled in an untidy crowd behind the Old Man, shouting and laughing at the tops of their voices so that every self-respecting animal fled as fast as its legs would carry it. The hunters found the whole spectacle quite embarrassing, and were glad that no other tribe was around to see it.

Before noon, they stopped in a large clearing and soon a magnificent picnic was under way. The Neanderthal folk ate and drank with gusto, wishing the Old Man "Good Health" and "Long Life and Happiness". After the feast, no one was really disposed to do much in the way of hunting. Not just yet, anyway. And, although the hunters fumed and fretted, the other grown-ups, including the Old Man, settled down for an after-dinner nap, while the children paddled in the stream and tried to catch minnows.

Late in the afternoon, the Old Man stretched and stood up. "I feel twenty years younger," he said. "How about this hunting, then? Have you found something for me to hunt? I think I could manage a sabre-toothed tiger or at least a deer."

The hunters looked at each other and made polite noises, none of them liking to tell the Old Man that

there was unlikely to be anything
bigger than a beetle stirring for miles.
Luckily, the Old Man wasn't really
expecting an answer. He waved his spear
to the crowd, who got to their feet and
followed him with a loud cheer back into
the forest. He was thoroughly enjoying
himself now. He held his spear at the
ready and occasionally held up his hand
for the people to stop. Then he put his
finger to his lips and said, "Sh!" and
everyone else copied him. Then on they
went, scanning the surrounding trees for
anything that might move. Then suddenly
the Old Man cried, "Look!"

No one could say exactly what it was
that the Old Man saw but already his
spear was flying through the air, up
through the branches and leaves

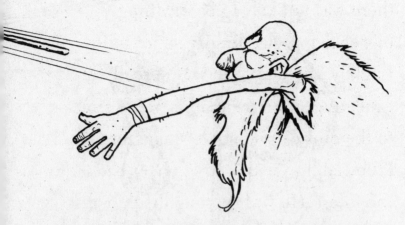

overhead. "Missed by a hair's breadth, Sir!" cried someone, although what it had been was still uncertain. What was certain, and without a shadow of doubt, was that the spear had not returned to earth. "It was an eagle. It's flown off with it!" cried another voice. But Littlenose, who had wriggled to the front, shouted, "No, it's stuck in a tree. High up."

"Do you think you could get it down, my boy?" asked the Old Man.

"I'll try," said Littlenose, and he

attempted to scramble up the trunk. But,
the bark was smooth and slippery, and the
spear could be seen, sticking out high
above the nearest branch. Littlenose came
back shaking his head. Several more
attempts were made but to no avail.

"We might as well leave it," said a hunter.

"It's time to go home and, anyway, it
was just an old spear."

"What do you mean, *old*!" exclaimed

the Old Man. "That spear is an heirloom! It was my father's, and his father's before that. I'll give a reward of five green pebbles to whoever can rescue my spear." There and then Littlenose made up his mind that the reward would be his. All the way home, he plotted and planned but, by the time they reached home, he still had no ideas. In fact, it was as he was dropping off to sleep that the first glimmerings of an idea came into his mind.

In the morning, Littlenose immediately remembered his idea for winning the Old Man's reward. He lay and thought a bit more, then Mum called that breakfast was ready, and he got up. Breakfast was almost over when Littlenose said, "I'm going to learn to fly."

Dad started to laugh. "What was that?

Fly?" he spluttered.

"Yes," said Littlenose. "Then I can get back the Old Man's spear for him."

At this, Dad fell off his seat and rolled on the floor, clutching his sides. "Oh-ho!" he cried. "Wait till I tell everyone. My son! Flying!"

Soon, every member of the tribe had heard of Littlenose's plan, and they laughed as much as Dad. It became a special joke, when someone met Littlenose, to flap their arms like wings and wink at him, so Littlenose quickly resolved to carry out his preparations well away from inquisitive eyes. In any case, people very soon got tired of the joke, except Dad. And he very soon was regarded as a bit of a bore on the subject of flying boys, flapping his arms and winking at everyone he met.

For his experiments in flying, Littlenose chose the part of the forest where the spear had been lost. It wasn't very convenient but he reasoned that, as soon as he had mastered the art of flying, he would want to waste as little time as possible. He started off by watching the birds. They just flapped their wings. And wings were really just sort of arms. So, Littlenose flapped his arms.

He flapped them standing still. And he flapped them running up and down. Nothing happened. His shoulders ached and he was out of breath but he stayed firmly on the ground. He watched some more birds. Of course, it must be the feathers that made the difference! He must get some.

For once, luck seemed to be going his way. There was roast goose for supper that night and the ground outside the cave was covered with feathers. Littlenose gathered two large handfuls of the biggest feathers he could find and hid them in his own special corner of the cave.

Next day started very early as Dad was going off for a day's hunting with some other men. It was barely daylight as Littlenose watched them making their way into the forest and, not long after, he too set off, clutching the goose feathers.

Littlenose was almost at the clearing when he heard voices. Carefully, he crept through the trees until he could see a group of figures. It was the hunting party! But they were not hunting. Far from it. They were sorting out a complicated system of rawhide ropes and talked as they worked.

"Do you honestly think that this is going to be any good?" asked one man.

"As good as anything anybody else has tried," replied another.

Dad spoke. "Nosey, here, had a good plan. He was just going to cut the tree down with his stone axe. But the Old Man wouldn't let him. Something about the tree falling on the spear and breaking it. Mind you, my boy Littlenose had the best plan.

He said he would fly up and get the spear."
He flapped his arms and laughed loudly,
although no one else did.

Littlenose was furious. The men weren't
hunting - they were after the reward! There
was no point in trying while they were all
messing around with ropes and things.
Angry and disappointed, Littlenose threw

the goose feathers away and went home. It seemed certain that the grown-ups would rescue the spear and earn the five green pebbles.

But things didn't quite turn out that way. Dad arrived home in the evening, and Mum said, "Had a good day in the forest, dear?" Dad said, "Hmph! Not a thing." And Littlenose's spirits rose. Whatever their scheme, the hunters must have failed; which served them right for being deceitful.

Then Mum said, "I hear the Doctor is planning to use magic to bring the Old Man's spear down from the tree."

Dad gave a short laugh. "Hah!" he exclaimed. "The Doctor can't even do the three pebble trick properly!"

Littlenose felt a little more optimistic,

and he began to think again. When people like Dad failed in something, they usually gave up. All that he had to do was wait for the winter gales, when the spear was certain to be blown down. He must make sure to be first there to pick it up.

So spring passed into summer and then came autumn. Littlenose visited the clearing from time to time, and still the spear remained where it was. In this particular clearing many of the trees bore fruit or nuts, and one autumn day Littlenose went off with Two-Eyes to pick some. There was a good crop, but one particular nut tree was loaded. There was only one problem. The nuts were high up, and the tree was so slender that when Littlenose tried to climb it, it bent and shook alarmingly. Next day, he went back, this time equipped with Mum's rawhide clothes line, which she didn't happen to be using just at that moment and wouldn't miss. He climbed as high as he could and tied one end of the rope firmly to the slender trunk. Then he scrambled down and gave the other end to Two-Eyes. Two-Eyes was small but strong and together they hauled on the rope until the tree bent down a little. Then they hauled some more. And again.

It took most of the day but, eventually, Littlenose and Two-Eyes sat back exhausted and admired the result of their efforts. The slender nut tree was now bent right down so that the topmost twigs touched the ground. The rope was tied to a handy tree stump, and they could gather all the nuts they wanted without

leaving the ground. But before they could
gather a single nut, there came an irate
shout. "Littlenose! What are you playing
at? No wonder there's no game. You've
scared everything away. Clear off!
Go home!"

It was Dad, followed by a hunting party.
Dad came towards Littlenose, paying no
attention to the tied-down tree, and started
to climb over it. Now, Littlenose's knots
were not very good at the best of times,

and Dad was half-way over when the knot fastening the rope to the tree stump gave way. There was a swish, a rustle, and a yell. The tree sprang back straight again. And Dad vanished. The hunters looked up in time to see Dad sailing gracefully into the tree-tops. He grabbed at a branch to save himself, but it came away in his hand and he came to earth in a briar thicket. There the others found him, scratched, bruised and dazed, and holding in his hand, not a branch . . . but the Old Man's spear!

Poor Dad! All the way home and for weeks after, everyone greeted him with flapping arms and a broad wink. They called him Birdman behind his back. Littlenose thought they were very unkind. At least, the Old Man had his precious spear back! However, he declared that, since no one person had rescued it, the reward should go towards the cost of another tribal outing in the summer. So everyone was happy. Except, perhaps, Littlenose, until one day the Old Man called him aside and gave him a special reward of a white pebble for himself. Which made up slightly for what happened when Mum discovered the state of her clothes line!

Littlenose and Two-Eyes

Littlenose sat under his favourite tree.
Two-Eyes was sitting beside him and, for
once, Littlenose paid no attention to the
little mammoth. Even when Two-Eyes
gave a squeak and prodded Littlenose
with his trunk, Littlenose brushed it aside
and said, "Don't bother me, Two-Eyes.
I'm busy, can't you see?"

Two-Eyes couldn't see, and he got

to his feet and went off in a huff.

Littlenose settled back against the tree, closed his eyes, and began mumbling to himself. He was learning a poem. It had all started a week ago. To everyone's surprise, not least of all Littlenose's, he had passed each of his tests for promotion from apprentice to junior hunter. Actually, he had one more test to do, which was the reason for the poem. He had passed fire-lighting with distinction, tracking with top marks, and spear throwing . . . just! But now he had the last and final test. It was called Hunting the Grey Bear.

There wasn't really a grey bear, or any other colour of bear for that matter. Three pieces of wood were tied together in a special way and covered with grey fur.

This was carefully hidden, and the apprentice hunter had to find it by following clues.

The clues formed a poem and it was this that Littlenose was memorising. It didn't seem to make a lot of sense, which didn't make it any easier to learn:

> *The Grey Bear's prints are in the clay,*
> *The noon-day shadow points the way,*
> *The island's where the heron cries,*
> *The ashwood close on willow lies,*
> *The peak where pine grows to the sky,*
> *The Grey Bear in his den does lie!*

Littlenose said it once through to himself, then once more out loud. As long as he remembered it tomorrow, all he had to do was work out what it all meant.

Next morning, Littlenose was up before it was light. After a quick breakfast, he hurried to the Old Man's cave carrying his boy-size spear. There was quite a crowd of hunters waiting to see him off. Dad wasn't there. He had gone off even earlier with another man to hide the Grey Bear. The Old Man made a short speech about how he hoped that Littlenose's name would be inscribed on the birch-bark roll of junior hunters. Then he gave Littlenose a tightly-wrapped package, food for the day "not to be eaten until the third line of the poem".

Littlenose took the package, said thank you, and set off while everyone shouted: "Good luck!"

As he left the caves behind, he was
quite sure of the first clue. The only clay
around was close to the river and was used
by the Neanderthal folk for making pots
and bowls. Sure enough, there was a line
of marks in the clay that looked more or
less like bear prints. As he looked, there
was a noise, and out from among the trees
trotted Two-Eyes.

"Go home," shouted Littlenose. "You can't come. This is all very important."

The little mammoth looked very crestfallen, and Littlenose turned his back and began to hurry along the line of tracks. The tracks left the clay but Littlenose found them easily as they crossed grassy patches, led through the pinewoods and took him far across a sandy heath.

Then they stopped. Just like that!

What was the next line of the poem?

The noon-day shadow points the way.

What shadow? Which way? It was almost noon now. He stood, perplexed. Then there was a quiet snuffle behind him. He jumped round.

"Two-Eyes!" he shouted. "What do you mean, following me like that? This is work for hunters, not mammoths!"

He started to think again about noon-day shadows, when Two-Eyes squeaked once more. He was standing pointing with his trunk to something on the ground. Right where the bear tracks ended was a rock. "That's no good," said Littlenose. "It's too sunken in the grass to cast a shadow." Two-Eyes pointed again with his trunk. The rock was chipped and cracked, and in the centre was a hole slightly bigger than a finger. "Of course," cried Littlenose. "You are a clever mammoth!"

He took his spear and stuck it upright in the hole in the rock. It was noon. The shadow of the spear lay along the grass, and at its tip was a white stone. A few steps away was another, then another. If he went from stone to stone

he should come to: *The island's where the heron cries.* He hoped it wasn't too far. He couldn't open his packed lunch till then, and he was getting hungry.

The white stones led in a wandering way over open country. Ahead, Littlenose could see low trees and bushes and the glint of water. As he got nearer, the ground underfoot grew damp. There were stagnant pools and clumps of reeds. He came to the end of the trail of white stones and found himself on the edge of a wide marsh. A broad, slow-flowing river lay across his path.

Littlenose and Two-Eyes splashed the short distance to the river. There were willow trees along the bank, and others growing on a couple of islands. Which was the island with the herons, he wondered? Two-Eyes nudged him with his trunk. Littlenose turned. A heron was pacing majestically through the shallows by the bank. It stood still for several moments, peering down into the water. Then , quick as a flash, its long beak darted into the water and came up with a wriggling fish. Littlenose watched. The heron slipped

the fish into its crop, then rose into the air on enormous wings. It circled round and dropped down into the top of a tree on the farthest-away island. "That's it," said Littlenose. "That's the one!"

Followed by a reluctant mammoth – Two-Eyes didn't like getting his fur wet – Littlenose waded into the river. The water was little more than knee deep, and they quickly reached the island. There were several heron nests in the trees, and the big birds screeched at the intruders.

"Well, the herons are crying, all right," said Littlenose. "That's the third line of the poem. Now I can eat my lunch." He opened the tightly-wrapped skin package. The Old Man had given him several pieces of prime venison. But . . . it was raw! It must be part of the test. All he had to do was build a fire.

It came as a nasty shock to find that there seemed to be nothing to build a fire *with*! The island was low-lying and swampy, and the few twigs and sticks Littlenose found lying in the grass were too wet to burn. Again, it was Two-Eyes who came to the rescue. He went over to one of the trees and reached up with his trunk. The branches were loaded with dead grass and sticks brought down in the winter floods, all perfectly dry. Littlenose stood on Two-Eyes' back and dragged down an armful. Quickly, he struck a light with his flints and, in a short time, the venison was toasting over the flames.

Fed and contented, Littlenose sat on a low willow branch and thought, while Two-Eyes grazed nearby. That was half the clues used up, although he had to admit that without Two-Eyes' help, he wouldn't have done so well! Why, if he weren't a mammoth, he might make a pretty good hunter himself. What was the next part of the poem?

The ashwood close on willow lies.

That wasn't much help. There was

plenty of willow. In fact, there was nothing else. Where did the bit about "ash" fit in? Was it perhaps among the driftwood in the trees? Oh dear! What if he'd burnt it in his cooking fire! He jumped down and picked up his spear. And as he did so, he remembered, the Neanderthal Folk used ash for spear and axe handles. It must mean his spear. Another thought struck him, and he climbed back on the willow branch. Yes! He'd wondered about the fresh marks cut in the bark. They were made just where small branches formed forks. He took the spear and rested it in the forks. It fitted perfectly, as if they were made for it . . . which they probably were! And the spear pointed straight back across the river towards a distant hill. That's where he had to go now.

The hill was farther away than Littlenose first thought and it was late afternoon before he came near its foot. It was really a small mountain. The lower slopes were quite bare – they seemed to consist of red gravel. Higher up was red rock. The rock formed weird peaks and pinnacles.

The peak where pine grows to the sky,
The Grey Bear in his den does lie!

And there, just visible against the sky, was the twisted shape of an ancient pine clinging to the summit of one of the pinnacles. There was the end of the trail. Somewhere up there were three pieces of wood tied together in a strange fashion and covered with grey fur. All he had to do was climb up and get it.

Littlenose strained his eyes to find an easy route to the summit. He paused. He could see people. Two figures seemed to be hiding behind one of the smaller pinnacles lower down. Of course! That would be Dad and his friend who had hidden the Grey Bear. He would pretend he hadn't seen them.

Littlenose and Two-Eyes circled round the base of the hill. And to their delight, they found that a path led almost to the top. Up they went, arriving panting close under the pine tree. It grew out of a crack above Littlenose's head, but the rock seemed quite impossible to climb. They stood precariously at the top of the gravel slope and wondered where on earth the Grey Bear could be hidden.

While Littlenose poked about, Two-Eyes

had been looking down to the foot. He gave a sudden soft squeak. "What is it?" said Littlenose. "Have you found it?"

He followed Two-eyes' gaze . . . and his heart almost stopped. Half-way up, a huge

black bear stood, rearing up on its hind legs.
It had been hidden from below by the
rocks. That was why Dad and his friend
were hiding! Not from Littlenose. The bear
took a couple of steps, but the gravel
slipped under its feet. It couldn't get at the
hunters, but it was prepared to wait!

"We must do something, Two-Eyes,"
said Littlenose. And he pulled himself up
on to part of the rock for a better view. Too
late, he realised that the rock was loose. He
flung himself to one side as the rock
crashed down the hill. He fell against Two-
eyes and together they rolled down after
the rock in a great cloud of red dust.

The bear leapt back in fright. What was
this? A landslide . . . and a cloud of dust
that made a noise like an angry mammoth!
To crown it all, a large rock bounced out

from the dust cloud just missing the bear's head. Without a backward glance, it turned and fled.

As the dust cleared, Dad and the other man ran to join Littlenose and Two-eyes. "That was one of the bravest things I've ever seen," said Dad. "And, of course, congratulations!"

Littlenose looked down. Brought down with the stones and gravel, and lying at his feet, was the Grey Bear.

That night, Littlenose stood proudly as the Old Man took a piece of charcoal and made the marks on the roll of junior hunters that meant 'Littlenose'. Dad whispered something in the Old Man's ear. The Old Man smiled and added: "and Two-Eyes".

"You two really are a team," he said.

"I knew Two-Eyes would make a hunter," thought Littlenose. Then he hurried home, hoping that being a junior hunter meant that he was now allowed to stay up late with the grown-ups.

The Amber Pendant

Next to the Old Man, who was Chief,
the most important person in Littlenose's
tribe was the Doctor. And this was not
only because he cured people when they
were sick, but because he was also a
magician! Everyone was a bit afraid of
the Doctor. Some said that he wasn't
Neanderthal at all. That was why he
never appeared without the ceremonial

mask which hid his face. Some even went as far as to say the he was really a Straightnose – which explained why he was so clever.

The Doctor's wife, Goldie, was even more of a mystery. By Neanderthal standards she was almost unbelievably ugly. Her hair was long and golden and her nose was not much bigger than Littlenose's. She rarely ventured from her cave, and people said that the Doctor was ashamed of her. Of course, they didn't say that to his face. You don't go around talking about someone whose husband could easily turn you into a frog or worse.

One evening, Dad came home and said, "The Doctor's wife has lost an amber pendant. He's offering a reward to whoever finds it."

Littlenose looked up from his supper. "I bet I find it," he said. "What's a pendant?"

"She wears it around her neck," said Dad. "Two pieces of amber on a leather thong."

"I see," said Littlenose. "And what's amber?"

Dad sighed. He thought for a moment. "It's yellow stuff. With flies in it. And it's magic."

Littlenose tried to picture it for himself. Yellow? Flies? All he could think about was egg yolk – with greedy flies getting their legs stuck. And magic? Magic egg yolk? He tried to imagine the Doctor's wife wearing two runny eggs covered with flies. Grown-ups were even odder people than he thought! But the reward! He didn't care

what he found as long as he got the
reward.

First thing after breakfast next day, he
set off with Two-Eyes to hunt for the
missing amber pendant. And it was a lot
more difficult than he had imagined.
Littlenose thought that all he had to do
was keep his eyes open for something
yellow. He said so to Two-Eyes. "Then we

check it for the flies," he said.

Two-Eyes sighed. Life with Littlenose was never dull, but it was sometimes hard for a young mammoth to understand what was going on.

They walked along by the river. People often lost things while they were fishing or just out walking, thought Littlenose. He peered at the ground and at the shallow water near the bank. Then he stopped. "Look, Two-Eyes!" he cried. Something bright and yellow shone among the small waves. He jumped down the bank. And saw that it was only the sunlight shining on the pebbles. Ah, well! Better luck next time!

Then it was Two-Eyes' turn. He gave a squeak and pointed with his trunk. In the shadow of a tree were two, bright yellow objects. Littlenose rushed to pick them up.

But before he had got half-way the two objects rose into the air and fluttered away among the trees. "Butterflies!" cried Littlenose. "You really are stupid, Two-Eyes!"

"He's a fine one to talk," muttered Two-Eyes in mammoth language, as they went on their way.

They came out of the trees into a wide clearing on the far side of which was a high outcrop of rock. And in the face of the rock was what looked like the opening of a cave. It looked promising as a place to find lost property. In any case, Littlenose liked exploring, despite the number of times he had been warned about going into strange caves.

Littlenose walked boldly into the dark entrance but Two-Eyes hung back. His mammoth senses told him that all was not well. Reluctantly, with a bit of persuasion, he followed Littlenose. And Littlenose had only taken a few steps when he stopped. At the back of the cave were two brightly-shining yellow objects. Littlenose could hardly believe his luck! It couldn't be the sun shining this time. And butterflies didn't live in caves. Then he paused. One of the yellow objects had disappeared for a moment. Almost as if it had blinked. "I must have imagined it," thought Littlenose. "This is certainly my lucky day!"

"This is certainly my lucky day," thought the sabre-toothed tiger. It had been having a quiet nap at the back of the cave when Littlenose had come charging in. Here, before its very eyes, was its favourite mid-morning snack: fresh, tender Neanderthal boy, walking straight up to it!

So as not to waste a moment, the sabre-toothed tiger opened its jaws wide, and waited.

Littlenose jumped as underneath the two bright shining objects appeared two rows of bright shining white teeth.

And as he grew accustomed to the dim light in the cave, he made out the shape of a sabre-toothed tiger! He was too terrified to move, even when the tiger rose to its feet and began to purr at the thought of fresh boy. Then it jumped back, startled. It hadn't seen Two-Eyes' dark fur among the shadows. But now the little mammoth

trumpeted as loud as he could. The echoes in the cave made it sound like a whole herd. And when the tiger saw a red eye and a green eye shining out at it, it didn't know what to think. Before it could make up its mind, Littlenose and Two-Eyes were out of the cave and running like the wind. They didn't stop until they were close to the caves where the tribe lived.

They knew the tiger would not pursue them there, so they sat down under a willow tree to recover their breath.

Littlenose put his hand on the ground and felt something in the grass. It was a rabbit's paw . . . but without the rabbit. Someone had taken the trouble to bind it round with strips of leather, and there was a loop as if it were meant to hang on something.

"Strange," thought Littlenose. "Perhaps Uncle Redhead will know what it's for." And he tucked it into the secret pocket in his furs.

But he was no nearer finding the amber pendant. "Come on, Two-Eyes," he said. "It will soon be lunchtime. Let's have one more look."

Littlenose started off, but it was marshy ground and Two-Eyes didn't like to get his

fur wet. He went the long way round.
Suddenly, Littlenose heard him squeal.
The little mammoth was standing, pointing
with his trunk. Littlenose ran to join him.
He couldn't see anything at first, but the
breeze stirred a clump of rushes and he
caught a quick glimpse of something bright
yellow. Again he splashed through the
pools of water. . . and found himself
looking at a clump of marsh marigolds.
The bright yellow blooms nodded in the
wind and made reflections in the water.

This was it, decided Littlenose. Reward or
no reward, he had had enough of lost amber
pendants. It was almost lunchtime. If he
could think of nothing better to do, he would
start looking again in the afternoon . . .
perhaps! Mum liked flowers, though, and it
would be nice to take a bunch back to her.

Littlenose picked a big bouquet of marsh marigolds and set off home.

He was almost there when he realised that he was close to the cave where the Doctor lived with his ugly wife. There was the cave, and someone was moving about outside. It was Goldie. She was preparing her husband's lunch, and sat on a rock in the sunshine plucking a pigeon. Littlenose knew that it was rude to stare, but he went closer and stopped to look at Goldie. She wasn't really all that ugly, even if she did have golden hair instead of the dark Neanderthal variety. And small noses weren't a total disaster, thought Littlenose, touching his own.

Suddenly, Goldie looked up. She smiled. "You're Littlenose, aren't you?" she said.

"Yes," said Littlenose, "and —"

"And you've brought me flowers!" cried Goldie.

"Well, really . . ." began Littlenose. Then he stopped and handed the bunch of marsh marigolds to her. "I've been out all morning looking for your amber pendant," he said. "And I haven't found it."

"I'm not surprised," replied Goldie. "It was never lost. The Doctor had no sooner offered the reward than I found it lying where it had fallen in a dark corner of the cave. I don't suppose he's got round to telling people yet. I'm sorry you were put to so much trouble. Would you like to see it?"

Littlenose nodded, not quite sure. Goldie went into the cave and came out carrying what looked like two large golden

pebbles strung on a leather thong. But they weren't pebbles. Littlenose could see right inside them.

"Take them," said Goldie. "Look at the insects trapped inside." Littlenose drew back. "Don't be afraid," said Goldie.

"What about the magic?" asked Littlenose fearfully.

"Oh that," laughed Goldie. "I'll show you in a moment."

Littlenose took the pendant in his hand

and held it up. True enough, there were several small flies and midges embedded in the amber.

Goldie took the pendant again and rubbed one of the pieces of amber vigorously against her furs. Then she held it over some of the small feathers plucked from the pigeon and, as Littlenose watched, the feathers floated upwards and clung to the amber.

"That's it," said Goldie. "Not very useful magic." Littlenose nodded in agreement. "Well I must get on," said Goldie. "A cavewife's work is never done. Thank you for calling. And for the flowers. Goodbye."

Littlenose was at his own cave when he remembered the rabbit's paw he had found. He must remember to ask Uncle Redhead about it next time he visited. He took it out of his pocket and was walking head down examining it when he bumped into someone. It was Nosey, the Chief Tracker of the tribe.

"Can't you watch where you're going?" he shouted. "You youngsters have no consideration! In my young day . . . hi! What's that you've got there?"

"I found it," said Littlenose.

"Clever lad! Clever lad!" shouted Nosey. "My lucky rabbit's foot! I've been lost without it! How can I ever repay you? Here!" And he thrust a handful of coloured pebbles at Littlenose, enough to buy all sorts of good things at the next market.

Littlenose stood deep in thought. What a strange day it had been! He had

almost been eaten by a sabre-toothed tiger,
looking for a pendant that wasn't lost. And
now he had a reward for finding a piece of
dead rabbit.

"Come on, Two-Eyes," he said. "Let's
see what's for lunch."

Rock-a-Bye Littlenose

Night had fallen and, in the caves of the Neanderthal Folk, everyone was asleep. Except Littlenose. He tossed and he turned. He sat up in bed and lay down again. "For goodness' sake, Littlenose," shouted Dad, "go to sleep! You're keeping everyone awake!"

This wasn't quite true, however, as Mum was only awake because Dad was shouting, and Two-Eyes was fast asleep in a corner.

"I can't get to sleep," said Littlenose. "My bed's full of bumps and wrinkles!"

"If you made your bed properly every morning as Mum tells you," said Dad, "this sort of thing wouldn't happen!"

Littlenose lay down and pulled the covers over his head and, surprisingly, was soon fast asleep.

When Littlenose woke next morning, he ached all over. "It's your own fault," said Mum. "You can spend this morning airing and shaking your bed and re-making it properly." A Neanderthal bed was a pile of bear skins and other furs, which served as both mattress and covers and was spread on the floor of the cave.

Littlenose began to drag his bedding out

into the middle of the cave. It was quite remarkable what came to light, and even more remarkable that he managed to sleep at all. There was an old flint knife and some lucky coloured pebbles in the fold of one fur. Lifting up another, an apple core and a couple of old bones tumbled out – the remains of a midnight snack. At the very bottom of the heap, a particularly hard

lump was revealed as a spare fire-making flint. It was exciting! Like a treasure hunt!

"Now," said Mum, get those furs outside and beat them until they are clean." And Littlenose laid out the furs on a rock and beat them vigorously with a long stick. He raised clouds of dust. When Mum was satisfied that the bedding was clean and fresh, Littlenose wearily carried it back into the cave to his own special corner.

Then he called to Two-Eyes and, together, they made their way to Littlenose's favourite tree where they did their more important thinking.

Littlenose said, "You know, Two-Eyes, people are pretty unreasonable. Sleeping on the floor, I mean. It's all right for you. With your fur, you could sleep on a bed of thistles without even noticing." He leaned back and watched a bird

disappear into the foliage above his head.
"Now, birds have more sense," he said.
"No lying on the hard ground for them;
they build nests with wool and feathers
and things to line them. And I bet they
never lose a single wink of sleep.

"Suddenly, he leapt to his
feet and shouted: "I'VE
GOT IT, TWO-EYES!"
Startled, Two-Eyes jumped
sideways and gave Littlenose
a suspicious look.

Littlenose's ideas usually spelt trouble for someone – more often than not for Two-Eyes. He sneaked away as Littlenose paced up and down waving his arms as he explained his great idea.

"People nests!" he said. "If people had nests like the birds, there would be none of this business of hard floors. At bedtime they would simply snuggle down and be lulled to sleep by the gently swaying of the branches." There and then, he decided to build a 'people nest', or rather, a 'boy nest' to prove that it could be done.

From the sun, Littlenose judged that it was almost lunch-time, but there was a lot he could do before then. He had to find a suitable tree, for instance. He set off into the woods.

He was deep in the forest before he

found what he was looking for. A tall straight tree with plenty of hand and foot-holds for climbing and, right at the top, a stout limb growing straight out from the trunk with a large fork at the end. He started to gather twigs and branches for his nest. The time flew past, and Littlenose forgot completely that he should have been home for lunch.

Then came the tricky part, getting the twigs and branches to the top of the tree and building the nest. Littlenose could only carry one branch at a time as he climbed carefully to the fork. Soon his limbs ached and he was scratched and sore. The branches seemed to get heavier and heavier but, in the end, the last one was up and carefully balanced with the others across the forked branch.

Then he took his flint knife out of his furs and carefully cut strips of bark about as long as his forearm and as broad as his finger. He began to arrange the nesting material across the fork, using the strips of bark to lash it firmly in place. Slowly the nest began to take shape. It was bowl-shaped and beginning to look very nest-like when he realised that he had run out of twigs. He didn't need many. Just enough leafy ones to make a soft and comfortable lining. He slid back along the branch to the trunk and broke off all the leafy branches he could reach and threw them into the nest. Then he hung down and collected more from lower down. It was a simple matter to arrange them inside the woven branches – and the job was done. Littlenose looked at his handiwork

with pride.
Carefully,
he lay
down on
the soft leaves.
He watched the
clouds drift across the sky.
The nest rocked gently in
the tree-top. And Littlenose
fell asleep!

When Littlenose didn't turn up
at lunchtime, Mum was angry. But
when there was still no sign of him
at suppertime, she became worried.
For Littlenose to miss two meals in
a row was most unusual. Dad came
home and a full-scale search was
mounted. With some reluctance
and a lot of muttering, the search

party assembled in the gathering dusk.

"If that boy were mine," grumbled one man, "I'd throw him to the bears!"

"They'd throw him right back," said another. "Bears have more sense!"

They were just leaving when a strange figure stumbled into the circle of torchlight. It was an old, old man. He carried a bundle of sticks in one shaking hand as he lurched and stumbled into the midst of the search party. He grabbed one man by the arm and wheezed and puffed, trying to speak and get his wind back at the same time.

"It's old Nod," said Dad. "What on earth's the matter with him?" Nod was a simple old man who spent most of his time collecting herbs. He had evidently been gathering firewood in the forest.

After a moment, Nod calmed down a

bit and stopped gasping. Then he pointed
dramatically back the way he had come
and cried, "Big as a mammoth! Out of the
sky! It'll have us all!"

"What will?" asked Dad.

"IT!" cried Nod. And he darted about
flapping his arms like wings and talking so

fast that only one word in ten made sense. Then they realised what Nod was telling them. He'd fled for his life from a giant bird! No, he hadn't actually seen a giant bird; but he had seen a giant nest! What more did they want?

"Could you lead us to it?" asked Dad. Nod was perhaps simple but he was not stupid. Bringing word of a ferocious giant bird in the forest was one thing – going back for another look was something else altogether. He gathered up his firewood and hurried off towards his cave.

"Silly old man," said Dad. "Probably imagined the whole thing! Come on. We've wasted enough time as it is." And off they set on their delayed hunt for the missing Littlenose. By the light of their torches, the search party peered into the shadows and

prodded the undergrowth
with their spears, but of
Littlenose there was no
sign. "You don't
suppose the giant bird
got him?" said someone.

"You don't believe that
nonsense, do you?" said Dad,
and he started to laugh. But no-
one else did.

The moon had risen and
Dad realised that the others
were not even looking at him.
They were gazing across a
clearing to where a
tall tree grew slightly
separate from the rest.
Their eyes travelled up
the trunk. Up and up to

where a large branch grew out near the top. And there they saw it. There could be no doubt. It was a nest. But what a nest!

"What do we do now?" they asked one another.

Littlenose woke with a start. He hadn't meant to sleep and now it was dark. He climbed out of his nest and slid along the branch to the trunk of the tree. He felt in the light of the moon for foot- and hand-holds. And there were none! Where were all the branches he had used to climb up? Then he remembered. The leafy branches he had broken off to make a comfortable lining were the very branches he had used. He was stuck. He got back into the nest, took a deep breath, and shouted: "HELP!"

To his amazement, there was an immediate reply. A voice out of the darkness shouted, "HI!" Then other voices joined in, including Dad's. They were all talking at once. Mainly nonsense, by the sound. "It's Littlenose! It must have got him! Do you think he's all right? Are you all right, Littlenose?"

"Yes," cried Littlenose. "But I can't get down."

"Hang on!" shouted Dad and, slinging a coil of rawhide rope around his shoulder, he began to climb the tree. He reached the last of the hand-holds, balanced himself as best he could, and tied one end of the rope around his waist. "Tie the end to the branch," he called, throwing the coiled rope to Littlenose. Littlenose did so and waited to see what Dad intended to do next. He never found out because, at that moment, Dad lost his balance and, with a horrible yell, vanished into the darkness. The search party scattered as Dad plummeted towards them. But the rope had got into a great tangle and Dad was brought up short half-way to the ground, dangling helplessly. "Don't all just stand there," he cried. "Get me down!"

"I'll get you down," came Littlenose's voice.

Dad looked up. "No, not THAT!" he cried.

Littlenose was clinging to the branch and sawing at the rawhide rope with his flint knife. "Almost there," he called encouragingly. And before Dad could utter another protest, the rope parted. For the second time, Dad hurtled groundwards. He collided head-on with one of the search party. Luckily, Neanderthal heads were made for rough

treatment. Even as they tumbled in a heap, another body crashed amongst them. Suddenly relieved of Dad's weight, the branch had sprung upwards, catapulting Littlenose into the air. The piled-up search party broke his fall safely, if a bit abruptly.

They got to their feet, picked up the scattered torches and looked at Littlenose. "Look at those scratches," they said. "Must be claw marks. Or beak marks. What an experience!"

Dad said, "We'd better not hang around in case it comes back." And off they hurried with Littlenose, not even scolding him for all the bother he'd caused. It was all very strange. Mum even burst into tears when he got home.

Still bewildered, Littlenose found himself washed, fed and tucked up in bed.

And of one thing he was now certain. Nests were so much trouble that anyone who preferred a nest to a good solid floor must be positively bird-brained!

Littlenose
the Hunter

JOHN GRANT
Illustrations by Ross Collins

Contents

Littlenose the Hunter

Littlenose was a Neanderthal boy who lived long ago, when people lived in caves and hunted animals for their food. When he grew up he was going to be a hunter like his father.

So, early one morning, Littlenose and Dad hurried off to an open space in front of the caves. All the hunters of the tribe and several other boys were there. A small stout man with white hair was in charge of the boys. He had been a very great hunter once, and now he was their teacher.

First the apprentice hunters were made to stand in a line while the teacher inspected their equipment.

Littlenose was carrying a satchel made of animal skin, and the evening before he had packed it very carefully with the things he needed. There was a clean pair of furs, a bundle of dried twigs, two flints, and a flint knife. And a brightly-coloured stone. He didn't really need the stone, but it was nice to look at.

Littlenose held his satchel out, trembling. The teacher raised one bushy eyebrow at the coloured stone, but nodded approval. Littlenose glowed with pride.

At last the party set off in single file. They followed the river to begin with, then crossed a ridge, and later a winding trail led them down into a thickly-wooded valley. At long last they halted in a wide clearing.

Dad and the other men didn't stop. They marched on across the clearing, and in a few minutes had disappeared. Then, one by one, the teacher called the boys to him. One was sent to catch fish. Another had to find fruit. A third was to look for bracken to make soft sleeping places for the night.

Littlenose was last to be called.

"Now, Littlenose," said the teacher, "I have a very important task for you. You will prepare our fire. Listen carefully. This clearing will be our camping place for the night. At sunset we shall require a good fire to cook supper. You must light a fire which is big enough to burn all afternoon. We don't want a great blaze, but a bed of hot ashes." Here he paused and wagged a finger at Littlenose. "If the fire isn't right, then that will mean a late supper, and hungry hunters are very impatient people. Now, it won't take you all day to build a fire. Everyone is going to gather on the other side of the hill, there." And he pointed. "At midday we eat, and then start lessons."

"Yes, sir," said Littlenose.

"I'll see you at midday, then, on the other

side of the hill. Just follow the path." And he strode off, leaving Littlenose all alone in the clearing.

Littlenose looked about him. He'd better get started. He made his preparations with great care. First, he gathered a pile of dry sticks, then took out the knife and the twigs and flints from his bag. He whittled the twigs into bundles of shavings, then struck the flints together, until sparks fell on them. Most of the sparks went out right away, but at last one stayed alight long enough for Littlenose to blow it gently. The spark grew brighter until it was a pale, flickering flame. Quickly he built more twigs into a pyramid over the flame, and blew again. Soon the twigs were crackling and spitting. He took out the coloured stone and admired it for a moment before putting all his things back in the bag. But the fire was supposed to be big enough to last until nightfall. Littlenose began throwing branches onto the flames. Soon he had to fetch more branches from the woods. The fire grew bigger and became higher and hotter. Littlenose wiped the sweat from his eyes. Surely *that* would be enough to last?

Littlenose took one last look at the fire, which was now making shimmering heat waves in the air, and followed the path into the forest. He could see the top of the hill behind which he was to meet the others, and the path led straight towards it. But soon it began to turn away to one side.

"This is no good," thought Littlenose. "I'll be quicker if I leave the path and make straight for the hill." And at first he was. There was very little undergrowth and walking was easy. He was quite close to the foot of the hill when he came to a sudden stop. There was water in front of him – it stretched black and smooth and deep-looking right to the bottom of the hill. This, of course, was why the path had not taken the straight route. Littlenose picked up a large stone and threw it. The stone fell with the hollow splash that stones make falling into deep water. He couldn't possibly get across here, and to go back to the path would take too long. He walked along the bank throwing stones.

He was beginning to think that the water sounded quite bottomless, when he paused. That last stone had sounded different. He tried another at the same place. It made the definite rattle of a stone falling into shallow water – shallow enough for him to wade to the other side. He splashed across, and in a few moments was safely on the other bank at the foot of the hill.

By the time Littlenose scrambled up the hillside and over the top to find the others, he was hot and tired. He was glad to sit down with the other boys and eat a lunch of cold grilled fish and berries. It was when he took out his knife to cut his fish that he made an awful discovery. His coloured stone was gone! But he hadn't time to look for it. Already the teacher was getting ready for the first lesson.

The boys were made to sit on a log and the teacher drew with a charred stick on the smooth surface of a large rock. He started off with a lecture on animal tracks. He sketched here, pointed there, and from time to time tapped on the rock with his pointer. He talked very rapidly in a high-pitched voice, and Littlenose began to feel more and more drowsy. He began to daydream of being such a fine hunter that he could go out before anyone was awake and be back with a rabbit, a red deer, a rhinoceros and an elk by breakfast time.

Littlenose sat up with a jerk. The teacher was speaking.

"Come along, now," he exclaimed angrily. "Surely *someone* can tell me what those tracks are. You, there!" And he nodded towards Littlenose.

Still half-dreaming, Littlenose blurted out, "Rabbit, red deer, rhinoceros and elk."

"Well done. Well done," exclaimed the teacher. "You seem to be the only one who has paid attention. YOU will be tracker on our hunt this afternoon. Who knows? You may even find us a rabbit, a red deer, a rhinoceros and an elk."

The men rejoined the party for the hunt, and Dad glowed with pride when he learned of Littlenose's success. Once more they formed a long line, but this time Littlenose was in the lead. "Come on, Littlenose," said the teacher. Littlenose held up his hand and waved the party forward. He led them under low bushes and branches until their backs ached, and made them squeeze through narrow spaces that bruised their ribs. The men soon realised that there were disadvantages in having a small boy as a tracker.

Actually, Littlenose had no idea where

he was going – he just reckoned that they were bound to see some sort of animal sooner or later, and then he could say that that was the one he was tracking. He led the party out into a clearing. He was hot and tired, so he held up his hand, and they all stopped. He put his finger to his lips, and the hunters held their breath and waited expectantly.

Across the clearing was a jumble of rocks. They looked shady and cool; Littlenose made his way towards them. The hunters tiptoed after him. They waited as Littlenose crept inside.

The next moment the hunting party scattered like leaves in the wind. Head over heels they tumbled towards the trees as, with an earth-shattering roar, there stepped out from among the rocks an enormous lion. It had been sleeping peacefully in the shade when Littlenose blundered in and fell over it. By the time the lion's eyes became accustomed to the bright light, there was not a hunter to be seen.

They ran and ran, straight down the hill. But they could still hear the lion roaring.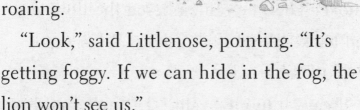

"Look," said Littlenose, pointing. "It's getting foggy. If we can hide in the fog, the lion won't see us."

Sure enough, a haze was drifting through the trees, and was beginning to form dense streamers between the trunks. In a few moments the hunters were only dim shapes in the mist. The next time they heard the lion roar it was a long way off. It had lost them. Again they stopped, and at almost the same moment everyone said, "This isn't fog!"

They had been so busy running that they hadn't noticed what their noses and smarting eyes now told them. It was smoke! It was getting thicker every moment.

"A forest fire," cried one man. "Run!" And he set off up the hill, away from the smoke. Then he remembered the lion, and ran back. "What shall we do? What shall we do?" he cried.

"Leave it to me," said Littlenose, and he began to climb a tall, straight fir tree. The smoke grew thicker the higher he went, but suddenly he came out of it, and saw blue sky above him. He also saw the fire. The whole forest seemed to be ablaze, particularly the site where he'd built the camp fire. The camp fire! He'd done it again! Well, they'd wanted a big fire! Anyway, it was too late to worry about that now. But there wasn't much time. They had to get away from the trees before they caught fire *and* avoid the lion. Littlenose hurried to the ground.

"Quick, follow me," he shouted. "Hurry!"

Again the hunting party scrambled along behind Littlenose. Only a few more paces, he thought; then he stopped dead. In front was a wide, dark and deep-looking stretch of water. They had circled round, and had reached Littlenose's earlier short-cut.

"We'll never get across. We're trapped!" the hunters cried.

"No, there is a way," shouted Littlenose. And he dashed along the bank, trying to recognise a tree or a bush or something which would give him a clue. Suddenly, everyone nearly fell over Littlenose as he bent down and picked up something from the ground.

"This is the place," he cried, and dashing into the shallow water he splashed his way to the far bank.

Littlenose looked at what he held in his hand. Wasn't it lucky that he had lost his coloured stone as he crossed the water the first time? If he hadn't spotted it lying in the grass, they would never have found the crossing place in time. In a few moments, the whole party was safe on the bare hilltop, while the fire raged in the woods. All night, the hunting party crouched in darkness,

watching the flames below. In the early
hours of the morning it began to rain, and
at last the sun rose on a soggy, sooty and
sizzling stretch of blackened woodland.

Black, wet, weary, and smelling of wood
smoke, Littlenose arrived home with Dad
late in the evening.

"It was all Littlenose's fault," said Dad to
Mum that night. "I know he saved us, but
it was only because of him that we *needed*
saving. Look at him, sound asleep there

without a care in the world."

Littlenose lay in a corner of the cave curled up under his fur covers. And in his hand he clutched a brightly-coloured stone.

Two-Eyes' Revenge

The cleverest and kindest person in the whole Neanderthal world was Littlenose's Uncle Redhead. At least, Littlenose thought so. He had already given Littlenose a flint knife, a picture of a beaver drawn on a piece of bark, and a set of pipes for making music. But, on this particular occasion, Uncle Redhead had been with the family for nearly a whole day and had so far given nothing to Littlenose.

It was evening, and Littlenose sat with his parents and Uncle Redhead around the remains of the evening meal. Everyone was too full to talk much, and soon Mum began to clear away the supper things. Dad bent over the fire, and poked it into a blaze. Uncle Redhead just sat with a faraway look. Littlenose just sat.

Dad was giving the fire a last poke when suddenly he leapt up with a yell.

"Ouch!" he shouted. "What was that? I've been stung!" And he rubbed his arm. Then he yelled again and jumped up, this time holding his ear.

"There are too many insects about," he shouted. "I'm going in." And he stamped angrily into the cave.

When Dad was out of sight, Uncle Redhead

almost fell off his rock laughing. He clutched his sides as he chortled into his beard. Favourite uncle or not, Littlenose thought him pretty heartless. After all, Dad had had two very painful stings, which was no laughing matter.

Mum came out of the cave on her way to the river carrying a large bowl. Uncle Redhead pointed to her, and suddenly there came a loud PING! from the bowl, which Mum almost dropped in surprise.

"Careful!" said Uncle Redhead, as Mum

went on her startled way. And again he doubled up with laughter.

Poor Littlenose was thoroughly bewildered. He turned to Uncle Redhead, but Uncle Redhead just said, "Time for your bed, young man. Pleasant dreams. See you in the morning." So Littlenose went to bed, a very perplexed boy.

In the morning, Littlenose tried desperately to ask his uncle about the strange happenings of the night before. But Uncle Redhead didn't appear to notice him, and chatted casually to Mum and Dad through breakfast.

However, when they had eaten, Uncle Redhead said, "Come on, Littlenose. Let's go for a walk. I still have to give you your present."

They walked off into the woods together, and there Uncle Redhead stopped on a grassy bank.

"Can I have my present now?" asked Littlenose.

"Just a moment," said Uncle Redhead.

He reached across and picked a thin, straight stick about the length of his hand.

"It's a berry-shooter," said Uncle Redhead. "It's a rowan stem, and, see, it's hollow."

But Littlenose still didn't understand.

With a sigh, Uncle Redhead took the hollow stick again, and putting a hand into a pocket, produced some red, wrinkled berries and put them in his mouth.

"Goodness, he *must* be hungry," thought Littlenose.

But Uncle Redhead did not chew the hawthorn berries. He put the berry-shooter to his lips, made a noise like "pfft!" and sent a berry shooting up into the leaves over their heads. Again and again and again he did it. "Pfft! Pfft! Pfft!"

"Oh, now I see," shouted Littlenose excitedly. "Let *me* blow one. *I* want to try."

Uncle Redhead gave him the berry-shooter and a berry. "Put the berry in your mouth," he said, "and put the berry-shooter to your lips. Take a deep breath."

Littlenose did as he was told. Then he gave a startled gasp. "I've swallowed the berry!" he gasped.

"That's all right," said Uncle Redhead. "I've plenty more." And he handed him another. This time, Littlenose got it right, and the berry popped out of the end of the tube and landed at his feet.

"Not bad," said Uncle Redhead. "Try again."

Littlenose tried again. And again. And again. In fact, he practised all afternoon, and by the time they set off for home he was getting very good.

"Now," said Uncle Redhead, as they approached the cave, "you must promise to be extremely careful when you are playing with your berry-shooter. I don't want you getting both of us into trouble."

When Littlenose awoke next morning, Uncle Redhead had gone. But tucked in amongst the furs under which Littlenose slept was the berry-shooter and a good supply of dried berries.

Littlenose couldn't wait to play with his new toy. He slipped a berry in his mouth and blew it towards Mum, who was busy preparing breakfast. But the berry flew over

her head and she didn't even notice it.
However, Littlenose remembered Uncle
Redhead's words about being careful, and
decided to wait until he was up and about
before trying again. As soon as breakfast
was over, he went to practise. But shooting
at leaves and flower heads was pretty dull.
He tried aiming at a fat thrush perched on
a branch. What Littlenose didn't see was a
wasps' nest hanging from the branch.
Instead of hitting the bird, the berry
smacked straight into the wasps' nest. Out
came the wasps, and off ran Littlenose as
fast as he could.

The wonderful toy was not turning out to
be as much fun as he had hoped. People
were much more interesting targets than
leaves or birds . . . or wasps' nests, for that
matter. After all, Uncle Redhead hadn't

actually *forbidden* him. He had only said to be careful. And he would be. Nobody had caught Uncle Redhead playing tricks with the berry-shooter, and they wouldn't catch *him*.

Unfortunately, Littlenose was not Uncle Redhead. He just wasn't cunning enough. He couldn't keep his face straight, and roared with laughter every time one of his hard berries hit someone on the ear or the nose, making them jump. It was not long before everyone in the tribe had been hit at least once; and one day some of the neighbours complained to Dad.

"Have you still got that berry-shooter?" he asked Littlenose, when they had gone. Littlenose nodded. "Right," said Dad. "Because it was a present, you may keep it; but you must on no account shoot it at people. One more complaint, and it goes in the fire. Right?"

"Yes," said Littlenose, very relieved that he still had his toy, but wondering what use it was going to be now.

At this moment Two-Eyes came ambling along. Two-Eyes! Of course! Why hadn't Littlenose thought of it before? He was Littlenose's best friend, but he wasn't "people". Not ordinary "people", anyway.

As Two-Eyes settled himself in a warm patch of sun to doze, Littlenose let fly with a berry. And Two-Eyes didn't move. Littlenose tried again. Two-Eyes didn't even look up. Then Littlenose realised that Two-Eyes just couldn't feel the hard hawthorn berries through his thick fur.

There was just one part of Two-Eyes which had no fur. The tip of his trunk. Littlenose took careful aim, and blew.

"Pfft!"

With a loud squeak, Two-Eyes leapt up. Littlenose blew again, and this time the berry hit Two-Eyes in the ear.

From that day on, Two-Eyes had no peace. He had only to show himself for a moment to find a stream of berries flying round his head. At length, thoroughly disgusted with things, he went off to stay with some friends, where, at least, he was safe from Littlenose and his berry-shooter.

When Two-Eyes had gone, Littlenose felt very sorry for himself. He had no one to shoot berries at, and he had no one with whom to do all the exciting things that he and Two-Eyes did together. He tried shooting at twigs floating in the river, and at fish swimming below the surface. But it was much too dull. Soon the berry-shooter was forgotten, and Littlenose wished that Two-Eyes would come back. And, one day, as summer was drawing to a close, Two-Eyes came trotting into the cave.

"Two-Eyes, you've come back!" cried Littlenose, happily. And he threw his arms around the little mammoth and hugged him. Once more, Littlenose and Two-Eyes played together. They explored the woods, paddled in the river, and invented games.

Littlenose had certainly forgotten the

berry-shooter. The Neanderthal folk had very short memories, and Littlenose's memory was shorter than most. But Two-Eyes was a mammoth. A mammoth not only *looked* like an elephant: like an elephant, a mammoth *didn't* forget. And a mammoth could be very patient indeed.

Summer was almost over. The leaves were beginning to turn red and gold. One morning, Littlenose called to Two-Eyes, "Come on, Two-Eyes, let's go and gather fruit." Together, they ran off into the woods, and in no time found all kinds of fruit, ripe and ready for eating. There were raspberries and blackberries and Littlenose gorged himself on those, and then he saw clusters of crab apples. He scrambled up the tree and threw down handfuls of the small apples. Two-Eyes picked one up, but immediately spat it out again. It was sour and unripe. Littlenose jumped down to the ground and ate several before he, too, decided that perhaps they were not quite ready for eating.

On another tree, dark clusters of elderberries showed among the leaves. Once again, Littlenose climbed into the branches and shook them. The tiny, dark fruits showered down onto the ground over Two-Eyes, who was waiting below. As they did so, an idea began to form in the little mammoth's mind. At last he was going to have his long-awaited revenge. Reaching down with his trunk, he began sucking up the fallen elderberries. Then he hid in a clump of bushes, and waited.

A moment later, Littlenose climbed down from the elder tree. He looked around him

. . . but there was no sign of Two-Eyes.
"Two-Eyes," he called. "Where are you?"

The reply he got took him completely by
surprise. Two-Eyes stepped out from
behind the bushes, took a deep breath, and
with his trunk pointed out straight in front
of him, sprayed Littlenose with elderberries.

"Oh! Ouch! Stop it, Two-Eyes," cried
Littlenose, his hands in front of his face.
But Two-Eyes didn't stop. He kept up a
steady stream of small, hard
berries until his trunk
was empty, and
then,
breathless,
but laughing
mammoth
laughter, he
ran off to

the river to wash the sticky elder juice from his trunk. Littlenose ran after Two-Eyes, but gave up after a short distance, and leaned against a tree to get his breath back. He felt rather dizzy. He didn't feel at all well. The woods seemed to be going round and round. He decided that it must have been the crab apples. Two-Eyes had sensibly spat his out. Why couldn't he have? Feeling very sick and dizzy, he made his way along the path towards home. It was dark when Littlenose reached the cave, and Dad was just thinking of going to look for him.

"Hurry up," called Mum. "I've kept supper for you."

At the mention of supper, Littlenose felt even worse. "Oh, no," he said. "I feel awful. I just want to go to bed." And he lay down in his own corner and pulled some furs over himself.

"What have you been eating?" asked Dad.

"Crab apples," groaned Littlenose.

"I might have known," said Mum. "You'll never learn. Let this be a lesson to you this time. You'll probably feel better in the morning."

In the morning, Littlenose woke, feeling well, and ravenously hungry. He bounced out of bed, but as soon as Mum caught sight of him she cried, "Get back to bed this minute!"

"I feel fine," said Littlenose. "Only hungry."

Mum had already shouted to Dad, who came running. He took one look at Littlenose. "What is it?" he said. "I've never seen anything like it. Does it hurt? Do you feel hot? Or cold?"

"I feel fine," said Littlenose. "I want my breakfast."

"Breakfast?" said Dad. "Don't tell me that

you feel fine, with spots like those."

"Spots?" said Littlenose, and he looked down. His arms and body were covered with a rash of purple-red spots.

"We must get the doctor," said Mum.

"No, we won't," said Dad. "All *he* does is put a fancy mask on, shake a lot of old bones over your head, charge five green pebbles, and tell you to stay in bed for a week. Tell him to see Auntie. She's bound to have medicine for this sort of problem, and she doesn't cost anything."

Auntie was a strange old lady who lived in a cave some distance from the others. Auntie always seemed to be ill herself, which Littlenose thought strange for someone who was supposed to be able to cure others.

When Littlenose and Mum arrived, Auntie was sitting by the fire with a fur rug over her knees.

First Mum had to give Auntie a lot of local news. It was mainly about people who had broken their legs, or had been eaten by something, or had been struck by lightning.

Finally, Auntie turned to the patient. She made him turn around. She looked in his ears and down his throat. Then she fetched a skin bag and a clay bowl from the back of the cave. She mixed something from the bag in the bowl with a little water and, handing it to Littlenose, said, "Drink. All of it."

It looked and smelt horrible, but Littlenose took a deep breath and drank. It tasted even worse than it looked or smelt, but he got it all down, coughing and spluttering so that he

spilt most of it over himself. He handed
back the cup, and wiped himself with his
hand. Then he saw the others staring at
him.

"It's working already!" cried Mum.

Littlenose looked down. Where he had
spilt the water, the spots were disappearing.
He rubbed some more, and they vanished,
leaving a purple stain on his fingers.

Wonderingly, he touched his fingers with his tongue. The taste was slightly sweet. He licked some of the spots on his arms. Yes. He knew what it was, and he laughed and laughed.

"It's elderberry juice," he shouted. "Where Two-Eyes shot them out of his trunk at me. I must have had the spots when I came home last night, but it was too dark to see."

A rather embarrassed Mum led Littlenose out of the cave after a muttered "goodbye and thank you" to Auntie.

But Littlenose paid little attention to either of them. He was hurrying home to have the biggest breakfast he could eat.

The Great Journey

At the time when Littlenose lived, almost
the worst thing that could happen was to
become ill. And this was because there
were no doctors in those days. At least,
there were no doctors as we know them. A
Neanderthal doctor wore a ferocious mask
and carried a stick hung with beads which
rattled when he shook it.

Instead of having his hand held and his

temperature taken, the Neanderthal patient was more likely to have magic signs painted on his forehead and the beaded stick shaken over him to drive away the sickness. About the only thing which was the same as today was that the medicine often tasted terrible! Some very odd things went into the making of it, although it was mainly herbs.

Now, despite all this, the doctor was a very important member of the tribe. He came somewhere between the Old Man and the Chief Hunter. One good thing about being doctor to a tribe was that other people had to work for him. It was supposed to be an honour. The most usual thing was to be sent to gather herbs to make the medicine. The women and children of the tribe were used to going out to collect the common herbs. But, for his most special medicines, the doctor required the leaves of the yellow bogweed which grew far, far away. Finding it was no job for women and children – it was work for the hunters.

One day, Dad came home looking irritable. The doctor had told him he needed more yellow bogweed.

"Oh no!" said Mum. "That only grows beyond the Great Moss. It will take weeks. Must *you* go?"

"Not only must *I* go," said Dad, "but Littlenose must come too. He is officially an apprentice hunter, and must take his turn with the rest."

At the mention of his name, Littlenose looked up. "What's that?" he said. "Are we going hunting again?"

"No. Gathering plants," said Dad, "for the doctor."

"Picking flowers!" exclaimed Littlenose. "That's girls' work. I thought I was learning to be a hunter."

"We are not going picking flowers," said Dad patiently. "We are going to one of the most dangerous places in the world. We must not only travel to the Great Moss, we must cross it. Only on the far side can we find the yellow bogweed."

"Can't we just walk round the Moss?" asked Littlenose. "Like we do the bogs on the moor?"

Dad flung up his arms. "Have you *no* imagination, Littlenose?" he cried. "The

Great Moss stretches far away on either side. No one has ever seen the ends of it. It takes days to cross from one side to the other."

"Cross?" said Littlenose. "You said I must never try to cross a bog. It's dangerous. I might be drowned."

"The Great Moss," explained Dad through gritted teeth, "is not just an ordinary bog. It is a huge swamp. It lies in the flat lands northward towards the Ice Cap. Parts of it are bog. Parts are almost dry land, with trees growing. There are streams and ponds, and thickets of reeds that you could get lost in. It is a damp, sad place, full of mist and the noise of water. Even the birds and animals sound unhappy. And, the land where the yellow bogweed grows is also the hunting ground of the Straightnoses."

Now, the Straightnoses were the deadly

enemies of the Neanderthal folk. They were tall, straight-nosed, and incredibly clever. Littlenose began to think that perhaps he would be better off doing girls' work picking flowers. The next few days were busy getting ready for the journey. Then, in the grey light of an early morning, they set off. Just before they started, Mum handed Littlenose a tightly-rolled skin bundle.

"I made this for you," she said. "Dad will show you how to use it."

Littlenose was puzzled, but he slung it on his back with his other gear, kissed Mum goodbye, and followed the men down the trail.

It was the longest journey which Littlenose had ever undertaken. And it was not only the longest, it was the most pleasant . . . at least to begin with. As they were not hunting animals, there was no need to look for tracks, and no particular need even to be quiet. The hunters trudged along in twos and threes, chatting, laughing, and occasionally singing. Littlenose chased butterflies, and threw his boy-sized spear at imaginary bears.

On the eleventh day after leaving home, the holiday came to an end. They had barely started their morning's march when one of the hunters pointed, and cried, "Look!"

Everyone looked. At first Littlenose could see nothing. The grassland they were crossing rolled away under a grey, heavy sky. There was no wind. Not even a blade of grass moved. Then Littlenose, peering where the man pointed, saw a thin line on the grey sky.

"What is it?" he asked.

"Smoke," said Dad. "A long way off."

"That means people," said another hunter.

"Either some of our own folk or . . ."

"Straightnoses!" gasped Littlenose.

"Exactly," was the reply. "And if we can see the smoke of their fire from here, then it must be a big one. This is no small party. This is a whole tribe on the move. One of ours. Or one of *theirs*."

"But," said Dad, "the Straightnoses don't usually hunt or travel in this part of the country. We shouldn't meet them until we've crossed the Great Moss."

"That just proves what I've always said," went on the first man. "The Straightnoses are unreliable. We must be on our guard from now on."

Luckily there were no emergencies during that night. They started off again after breakfast, and it was not long before Littlenose began to sense that something was different. The sky was still grey, but seemed lower. The air was definitely colder. They were now walking on damp grass, and ground that sometimes squelched underfoot. They passed stagnant ponds, and often they had to wade through long stretches of shallow water.

Two days later, towards late afternoon, Dad pointed ahead. "There they are," he said. "We'll soon be there."

"There are what?" said Littlenose.

"The trees," said Dad. "We'll make our last camp there before crossing the Moss. This is just the edge of it. Tomorrow we do the difficult bit."

Littlenose looked ahead, and could just make out a dark blob in the mist. The trees, when they reached them, turned out to be a group of ancient willows. They grew on a little island of raised ground, but even here the earth was damp and chilly. Dad came over to him.

"You must be very careful, now, Littlenose,"

he said. "And do exactly as you are told. First, hang your things up clear of the ground."

Littlenose did this, slinging his gear from a stump of tree branch.

"Now," continued Dad, "you are Fire Boy. You must get a fire lit while we work."

Littlenose wondered what the work could be, but he set about collecting firewood. Most of it was damp, and some of it was very wet. At first the fire was all smoke, but gradually, some flames appeared.

The men finished their work. One had been fishing, and a fine fish supper was set grilling over the fire. The others, however, seemed to have been doing something very strange. They had cut bundles of long, straight willow twigs which they had then stripped of their bark. Littlenose wondered of what use they could possibly be, but

before he could ask, someone shouted,
"Time to eat!" Some of the men stood to eat.
Some squatted. Nobody sat – the ground
was too wet. Littlenose wondered where they
would sleep.

The meal over, Dad said, "We've a hard
day ahead of us tomorrow. It's time to get
some sleep."

"On the wet grass?" asked Littlenose.

"No, in our hammocks," replied Dad.

"But I haven't got a hammock, whatever
that is," said Littlenose in a bewildered voice.

"Yes you have," said Dad. And he lifted
down the bundle which Mum had given
Littlenose. Dad untied it, and Littlenose
saw that it was a long wide strip of skin
with rawhide ropes at each end. Dad tied
the ropes on one end to the trunk of a tree.
Then he stretched out the skin and tied the

other end to a second tree. The skin now hung clear of the ground.

"That," said Dad, "is your hammock. Get in." And he lifted Littlenose up. The hammock swung gently, and was very comfortable indeed. Across the glade, other hammocks were being slung, and in a few moments the whole party was snug and dry and calling "Goodnight" to one another.

Littlenose looked up. A few stars had appeared. As he watched, the stars seemed to blink. He watched, and they did it again.

"How very odd," he thought. Then he saw why. The hammock was swinging gently, and he was seeing the sky through the branches of the willow tree. It was the twigs and leaves coming in front of the stars that made them seem to blink. Littlenose wriggled so that the hammock

swung faster. This was fun. He swung faster
and faster, while the stars blinked and winked
furiously. Then he swung just a little too
far. With a yell and a thump he tumbled to
the ground. Immediately, the camp was in
an uproar. Men grabbed for their spears,
and Littlenose found himself in the middle

of a circle of very unfriendly faces.

"I fell out," he said.

"You were fidgeting," said Dad. He lifted Littlenose back into the hammock and wagged a finger at him. "One more piece of nonsense from you, and you sleep on the ground. All right?"

"All right," said Littlenose, and he lay down and fell fast asleep.

The hunters set off very early next morning. Each man carried his spear and a small bag to hold the special leaves for medicine. In addition, each held a bundle of the peeled willow sticks. The hunters moved in single file, and quickly reached the edge of the Great Moss. It was just as Dad had described it. A sad, lonely place; just marsh and bog. The line of hunters stopped and then started again. Littlenose, bringing up the rear, saw one of the white twigs sticking upright in the soft ground. Dad called back to him, "Keep to the line of sticks, otherwise you will be drowned. We must feel our way across, and these will show us how to get back."

Peering ahead, Littlenose could see the leading hunter prodding the ground carefully in front of him with his spear. Only when he found firm footing did he move forward. Every so often, he stuck in a willow twig to mark the route, and slowly and steadily the little party zigzagged its dangerous way across the Moss. Behind them, a winding line of white sticks showed where they had passed. Half the day was gone before the last stick was pushed in, and they were walking on dry turf up a gentle slope.

After a pause for a rest and something to

eat, the plant picking began. The yellow flowers of the bogweed were easy to spot, but it was the thick fleshy leaves which the doctor required. It was back-breaking work. Littlenose was luckier than the others in that he didn't have so far to stoop. All the same, he was glad when he had filled his bag with leaves and could straighten up. He looked all around. It was a very depressing spot. Then a movement caught his eye. It was near a low ridge of land a short distance off. Was it a large animal? A mammoth, perhaps? He saw a line of small shapes, dark against the grey sky.

He watched for a moment longer, then dashed over to Dad.

"Look," he said, pointing.

Dad looked, dropped flat into the grass and whistled softly. At his signal, the others

174

also dropped into cover, and watched where
he pointed. The shapes were coming closer.
They were men. Tall and erect, carrying
spears, and getting nearer every moment.

"Hunters," said Littlenose.

"Straightnoses," said Dad. "We must get
out of here fast."

"When I give the word," whispered the
leader, "make a run for it. Follow the
willow twigs. Don't try taking short-cuts."

He took a last look towards the
Straightnoses, then shouted, "NOW!" and
raced helter-skelter for the Moss. The rest

followed. Littlenose found himself bringing up the rear once again, as he slipped and stumbled over the quaking ground from one stick to the next. They were well into the Moss before they paused for breath. Then they had a terrible surprise. Neanderthal people were not very bright, and they had imagined that crossing the Moss would somehow bring them to safety. But, to their horror, the Straightnoses were doing as they were, and following the sticks. In panic, the hunters fled on. Except Littlenose, that is.

"How silly can we get?" he thought.

Running to the nearest twig, he pulled it out, then he ran after the hunters, pulling out each twig as he came to it, and throwing it into the Moss so that no one could tell where they had been.

Very quickly a gap grew in the trail.
When the Straightnoses reached the last
willow stick they shouted with rage. One
tried to dash after Littlenose, and was only
saved because another grabbed him by the
hair as he sank into the marsh. A
Straightnose threw a spear which hit the
ground behind Littlenose with a plop and
vanished.

Disappointed, the Straightnoses turned
back towards solid ground.

When the Neanderthal hunters reached

their camp, Littlenose was treated as a hero. After all he had saved them from the Straightnoses. He was allowed to sit in his hammock *and* swing in it, while the fire was made by one man and his supper brought to him by another.

When they reached home, many days later, he was again treated as a hero. Littlenose wasn't sure how long it would last but one thing was certain – he was going to make the most of it!

Littlenose the Fisherman

Although Littlenose was an apprentice hunter,
and often went with the men of the tribe to
hunt, the Neanderthal folk didn't eat meat
all the time. They had wild fruit, roots and
bulbs, nuts in the autumn, and honey in
the summer. And in spring, when the ice
had vanished from the ponds and streams,
the Neanderthal folk became fishermen.

One day, Littlenose's father announced

that it was time Littlenose was taught to fish.

"But he can't keep still!" said Mum. "He's so noisy every fish will disappear when Littlenose reaches the river."

"I know," said Dad gloomily, "but he must learn. Starting tomorrow."

Neanderthal fishermen needed to be very quiet and patient as well as skilful. They would crouch by the river bank or wade into the shallows, stay very still, and when a fish appeared lunge down with their special fishing spears.

First Dad tried to teach his son how to use a fishing spear on dry ground. But Littlenose became confused and managed to spear his own foot. It didn't hurt much, luckily, because he'd made such a bad job of sharpening the spear.

Next day Dad took him on a real fishing

trip. All morning Littlenose waited quietly and watched Dad, who was patient and careful, and, one by one, caught six trout.

"Now it's your turn," said Dad. "Do as I did, and you can't go wrong."

Littlenose lay on the bank until his head and shoulders were over the water and took a firm grip on the spear.

"Whatever you do," whispered Dad, "don't let go of the spear."

Littlenose waited; a fisherman must have patience. He peered into the water until a wide open mouth and dark body shot towards the surface. Then he plunged downward with his spear as hard as he could. Too hard! He lost his balance and, with a yell and wildly-kicking legs, fell headlong into the water.

Calmly, Dad caught him by the hair and

pulled him onto the grass. It was minutes
before Littlenose could recover his breath.
Then he held up the spear and said
proudly, "I didn't let go!"

Back at the cave, Mum wrapped
Littlenose in a warm fur rug, while Dad sat
muttering to himself.

Suddenly, Littlenose looked up. "Dad,"
he said, "I've been thinking."

Dad laughed. The idea of Littlenose
thinking was very amusing. Mum was

somewhat taken aback, too, but she said, "Go on, Littlenose. Tell us."

"Well," said Littlenose, "Dad went to a lot of bother just for six trout. I've got a better idea."

"I suppose you could do better," snorted Dad. "Let's hear this wonderful idea, then."

"Catch bigger fish," said Littlenose.

"Eh?" said Dad.

"Yes," said Littlenose. "If those trout had been six times as big you need only to have caught one."

Dad sat for a moment with his mouth hanging open then he laughed and laughed. The tears rolled down his cheeks. He couldn't speak. "Oh ho!" he shouted. "All we need is one giant trout and our troubles are over!"

"Not trout," said Littlenose. "Salmon."

Dad stopped laughing. "Now you're not being funny," he said. "Just plain silly."

"No, I'm not," said Littlenose. "We've had salmon to eat before."

"Just think for a moment," said Dad. "Every spring the salmon pass up the river from the sea. You've seen them. They're as big as you are. They leap and race through the water as fast as a galloping buffalo. They stay right out in the deep water. They don't come near to the surface waiting to be speared. They're much too clever! The ones we've eaten were injured and washed up on the sand. Nobody catches salmon."

"But Uncle Redhead told me . . ." began Littlenose.

"Uncle Redhead tells you far too much," said Dad. "Mainly nonsense!"

Dad didn't care much for his brother-in-law. He thought he was more clever than was proper in a Neanderthal man.

"Uncle Redhead says," continued Littlenose, "that the bears catch salmon. Upstream the river becomes very rocky, with rapids and little waterfalls. The bears wade out to the rocks and catch the salmon as they rest, or as they jump clear of the water. Uncle Redhead says the ones we get are those that the bears couldn't keep hold of and that are washed downstream by the current."

Dad said nothing for a moment, then he nodded his head wisely. "All we have to do, then, is grow claws like the bears, wade into the river and pick out as many salmon as we need. Littlenose, you're impossible!" And he walked out of the cave in disgust.

"Never mind, dear," said Mum. "I think it's

a perfectly lovely idea, but it's time for bed."

Littlenose spent most of the night lying awake thinking. Dawn was breaking when he did fall asleep, but by then his plans were made.

No one mentioned fishing at breakfast, and when Littlenose strolled out of the cave with Two-Eyes his pet mammoth, Mum didn't even notice that he was carrying his hunter spear and some food. Littlenose had given a lot of thought to the matter of a spear. Fish spears were light and delicate for catching small fish, but to use one on a salmon would be like throwing stones at a woolly rhinoceros. Littlenose had his own spear, a real hunting spear, but boy-size.

Littlenose decided that Two-Eyes had better come to help him carry his catch. Even one salmon was likely to be too big for Littlenose.

Soon Littlenose and Two-Eyes had left the caves behind, and were in strange country. Few of the tribe ever ventured farther than this, and Littlenose imagined that any moment he would come to the place where the bears fished.

The sun rose higher, Littlenose trudged on, and still the river flowed wide and smooth.

At midday he stopped by the water's edge and had a picnic. Even as he sat and ate, salmon could be seen far out in the river. The great fish were leaping head and shoulders out of the water and falling back in showers of spray. The sun glinted on their scaly bodies, and Littlenose wondered how he could ever hope to catch one. But sitting looking wasn't going to do much good. If he didn't reach the rocky place soon he would have to go home empty-handed.

The afternoon wore on.

Littlenose and Two-Eyes were by now very tired. Several times they had to leave the river bank to make their way around the cliffs and marshes, and Littlenose hoped that they hadn't missed the bears' fishing place. But soon he realised they were not going to reach their destination that day, and it was too late to go home. There was only one thing to do. He found a sheltered corner between two rocks, and lighting a fire with his flints to keep away wild animals, he snuggled down against Two-Eyes' shaggy coat for the night.

Littlenose woke with the birds' dawn chorus, and had the remains of his meat. Two-Eyes ate some grass, then the two of them continued their journey. The river swung round a bend at this point, and as they turned the corner Littlenose cried, "Look, Two-Eyes!"

Below, the river narrowed, and in the gap between the banks were several large rocks around which the water swirled and frothed. As they watched, a salmon leapt high out of the water, over the rocks, and into the smooth river upstream. Then another salmon splashed its way up one of the small waterfalls, almost completely out of the water.

Without wasting any time, Littlenose climbed down the bank and made for the slippery rocks, while Two-Eyes watched. By the time he reached the middle of the river he was breathless. He found a rock that was fairly flat, and carefully stood upright. Gripping his spear, he waited. Nothing happened. There were no salmon. The last one must have gone!

Suddenly a movement caught his eye. There were salmon all around him! Only the occasional fish leapt above the rocks. Many more were swimming through the channels between the boulders. Looking down, he could see huge dark shapes weaving their way past the rocks. Now and again one would break the surface, and Littlenose had a glimpse of large eyes and great hooked jaws.

He waited no longer. Trying to remember all that Dad had told him, he gripped his spear firmly, took careful aim, and struck downwards with all his strength.

A jarring shock almost broke his arm, and next moment he was in the river. He clung on to the spear as it was wrenched this way and that. He was buffeted and bruised by a large tail and dragged hither and thither through the water. Then he was clutching something, and the river was carrying him along, sometimes on top, but more often under the surface.

It seemed hours later that Littlenose felt sand under him. He shook the water from his eyes and staggered ashore . . . dragging behind him the most enormous salmon. It was quite dead, and he could see where his spear had struck, but of the spear itself there was no sign. There was also no sign of Two-Eyes. He would have to get his fish home all by himself.

Meanwhile, back at the caves, a search party had just returned.

"There's no sign of him," said the leader. "We can't think of anywhere else to look. Do you have any ideas?"

"No," said Mum, sobbing, "he was such a good boy, never any trouble."

"Probably been eaten," said a neighbour. "It's always happening." He broke off as one of the hunters ran up.

"This has just come down with the current." He held out a boy-sized hunting spear.

"It's Littlenose's," wailed Mum. "He was talking of catching a salmon, and now they've eaten him."

For the rest of the day, the tribe watched

the river as if waiting for Littlenose himself to come floating by like the spear.

"If only he hadn't gone off by himself," they said. "There wasn't a nicer boy in the whole tribe. He was so kind! So generous! Always willing to help. Never disobedient. An example to everyone."

Their hopes were raised when late in the afternoon Two-Eyes came wandering along, for usually when he arrived Littlenose was not far behind. But when night fell there was still no sign of Littlenose.

Suddenly, the silence was broken by a voice shouting, "Hi! Come and help me, somebody!"

The tribe poured out of their caves, wondering what all the fuss was about.

A small figure, dripping wet and covered

with mud and fish scales, was dragging
something heavy along the river bank.

"Littlenose!" they all screamed. "Where
have you been? We've been worried sick.
You're a wicked inconsiderate boy, with no
thought for others. You ought to be thoroughly
ashamed." They calmed down a bit when
they saw the huge salmon, but went off
muttering about modern youth.

Mum cried a little. Then she washed

Littlenose and tucked him up in bed.

Dad carried the salmon into the cave, and, do you know, by the end of the week Littlenose didn't like salmon any more!

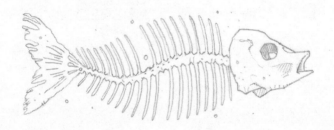

Littlenose's Holiday

Littlenose was bored. He scuffed the sandy floor of the cave with his feet. He sighed and picked up a twig and started to whittle it, then threw it into the fire and sighed again.

"For goodness' sake, stop fidgeting," said Mum. "Go out and play. It's a beautiful day."

"I've nothing to play at," said Littlenose.

"Play with Two-Eyes," said Mum.

"He doesn't want to play. He just wants

to sleep," said Littlenose.

"Well, go out and play by yourself," said Mum impatiently. "In fact, just go before you drive me completely mad!"

Wearily, Littlenose rose and dragged himself out into the sunshine. What could he do? Climb a tree? Climb one, he thought, and you've climbed the lot. Paddle in the stream? Last time he had fallen in and had been scolded for getting his furs wet. Idly, he picked up a broad grass blade, held it flat between his thumbs, and blew. It made a squeaking noise. Littlenose brightened up. He picked a better grass blade and blew harder, then again and again. His boredom forgotten, Littlenose took an enormous breath and blew with all his might, making a wild shriek that was pure joy to his ears.

Next moment he was
knocked sideways
by a hard cuff on
the side of the head.
Dad stood over him.

"What do you think
you're doing?" he shouted.
"Disturbing the whole
neighbourhood like that!"
Dad took Littlenose by
the ear and marched him away from the
caves. "If you must make that ghastly
noise," he said, "at least make it where we
can't hear it." Then he went back to
apologise to the neighbours.

Littlenose dropped the blade of grass.
There didn't seem much point in it now.
Anyway, he might as well do something
useful, like practising fire lighting.

He collected a handful of twigs and dry leaves, and after only three attempts managed to catch a spark on one of the leaves. The fire soon crackled briskly, and Littlenose glowed with satisfaction.

Now he thought he would try something more difficult. When hunters were troubled by flies and midges in their camp they made a smudge, a very smoky fire which drove insects away. The trick was to put green stuff onto a fire without actually putting it out.

Littlenose piled on handfuls of grass and the smoke began to get thicker. Soon it was coiling in dense wreaths. He kept adding more greenery, and from time to time he knelt and blew into the heart of the fire just as he had seen the hunters doing. Soon it was lunch time and Littlenose decided to hurry home before he got into more trouble.

Mum was very relieved when Littlenose arrived, smelling a bit smoky, but smiling. They were just finishing their meal when there was a cough, and one of their neighbours appeared. He shuffled his feet, cleared his throat and said, "I don't want to complain, but could I have a word with you for a moment?"

Dad nodded, and the man came in, followed by his wife.

"It's like this," said the man. "The wife, here, washed her best white fur wrap and hung it on a bush to dry, and it seems that your boy, there, was lighting fires or something. Anyway, he was making a lot of smoke and, well, have a look for yourselves."

The woman held out a grey, grubby piece of fur. It was spotted with what seemed to be soot, and couldn't have looked less like a best white fur wrap. Moments later,

Littlenose was in bed in disgrace, Mum was offering to re-wash the fur wrap, and Dad was vowing to feed his son to the first black bear that snuck its nose out of the forest.

Before going to bed that night, Dad was in despair. "I wish I knew what to do with Littlenose," he said. "He's more trouble than a whole herd of woolly rhinoceros."

"I thought you were going to feed him to

a black bear," said Mum.

"Attractive as the idea is," said Dad, "it is illegal."

"I'm sure you'll think of something," said Mum.

Next morning at breakfast there was suddenly a cheery shout from outside. Littlenose brightened up immediately. "That's Uncle Redhead," he cried.

Sure enough, the stocky figure of his uncle could be seen coming up the path. He waved. "Any breakfast left?" he shouted.

"If you hurry," called back Littlenose, as Mum hurried out to greet her brother. Dad didn't come out.

After Uncle Redhead had eaten, he said, "I really came here to ask you a favour."

Father looked at him carefully and said, "Mm."

"It's like this," said Uncle Redhead, "I've some business to take care of here, and I could do with help. A sort of camp boy to fetch and carry, and to light the fire. Do you think that Littlenose could be spared for a couple of weeks?"

Dad leapt up and shouted with delight: "Two weeks? You can have him for two months if you want."

When Littlenose heard that he was to go with Uncle at first he was too thrilled to speak. Then he hugged his uncle and demanded, "When do we go?"

Littlenose and Uncle Redhead left in the early afternoon, and by sunset were far from home. Littlenose was busy lighting a fire under a big tree, and Uncle Redhead had gone off to catch some fish for supper. Soon four fish were grilling over the flames.

When they were eaten, to Littlenose's delight, Uncle Redhead brought out from his pack two pieces of honeycomb dripping with honey.

Littlenose had never had so much honey at one time before. He sat munching before the fire while his uncle told marvellous tales of the strange places he had visited and exciting things he had done. Littlenose hoped they were going to do something exciting on *this* journey.

Soon it was time for bed, and after building up the fire to keep away wild animals, they settled down for the night. For a while Littlenose lay awake and wondered what they would do in the morning. What did happen came as a shock.

He was wakened by shouting. "Wakey, Wakey! Rise and shine! Show a leg! The sun's burning your eyeballs!"

Littlenose opened one eye. The sun was barely over the horizon, and the air felt chill. He snuggled down under his fur covers, but they were pulled off by Uncle Redhead.

"Come on now, time's a-wasting. Follow me," he shouted, and ran off at a rapid jog-trot. Littlenose got up and followed. He was soon out of breath and had a stitch in his side. Then, to Littlenose's relief, Uncle Redhead stopped and waved him on. They were beside a broad stream.

With a cry of "Last one in's a woolly mammoth!" Uncle Redhead threw off his furs and leapt into the icy water. Littlenose was horrified. He stared as his uncle splashed about calling, "Come on in, the water's lovely!" Slowly, Littlenose took off his furs and stood on the edge, goose-pimply and shivering. He stuck one foot timidly into the water. With a shout of glee, Uncle Redhead grabbed his ankle.

Next moment Littlenose was gasping and spluttering in the icy stream. He made for the bank, missed his footing, and fell headlong.

"That's the stuff," said Uncle Redhead. "Get the water right over you. Enjoy yourself! I always look forward to my morning dip."

All Littlenose was looking forward to was getting out of the freezing water.

Littlenose felt warmer, if completely breathless, by the time he had run to camp. Uncle Redhead was already cleaning some fish. "Hurry up with the fire, Littlenose," he said, and Littlenose blew the smouldering ashes into a flame. The fish were quickly cooked and eaten, and afterwards Uncle Redhead again gave him a huge piece of honeycomb. Fed and dry and glowing all over, Littlenose thought that perhaps life with Uncle Redhead wasn't too bad after all. He stretched out beside the fire, feeling pleasantly drowsy. But not for long.

"Mustn't hang around," said Uncle Redhead, kicking sand onto the fire to smother it. "There's work to be done." Before Littlenose realised what was happening they were on their journey again.

Uncle Redhead walked with long strides

which made it difficult for Littlenose to keep up. He hummed and whistled as he went, and from time to time burst into song. Or else he started long conversations. But Littlenose was too breathless to do more than whisper the occasional reply. They stopped briefly at noon for a quick snack of fruit and honeycomb. Littlenose was too tired to ask where they were going. He just trudged behind his uncle, who laughed and sang as merrily as ever, and never seemed to get tired at all.

At long last they stopped. They were on the shores of a small lake, and made their camp by a clump of pine trees. Littlenose flopped wearily to the ground. But it was his job to make the fire.

By the time that the fire was burning up, Uncle Redhead had come back with two fat rabbits. Quickly he cut them up and set them to roast over the flames. Littlenose ate his share with relish. He sat back, full, and his uncle grinned and said, "Now here's the bit you've been waiting for, isn't it?" And he handed Littlenose a piece of honeycomb. Littlenose groaned. He thought he would burst, but somehow he managed to chew and swallow the sweet, crunchy wax.

That night again Uncle Redhead laughed and chuckled his way through the same old stories, occasionally breaking into song. Littlenose just wanted to sleep. He began to think how nice it would be if his uncle would only be quiet for a while! At long last he said goodnight and pulled the covers over himself. Thankfully, Littlenose settled down to sleep too, without much success. Uncle Redhead even talked in his sleep. He muttered to himself, and from time to time let out a guffaw of laughter.

Yet that was not the only thing keeping Littlenose awake. He remembered the dip in the icy stream, and dreaded the morning. There seemed no way of getting out of it, and at last he fell asleep determined to show Uncle Redhead that he was tough too.

It seemed only a moment later that he heard: "Wakey! Wakey! Rise and shine!"

Without a moment's hesitation, Littlenose was out of bed. Down the beach he ran, off came his furs and he hurled himself into the lake. He landed with a thump. The water was only a few inches deep and the bottom was black, smelly, mud!

Littlenose sat among the slime, while

Uncle Redhead roared with laughter. "If I'd known you were so keen on bathing I'd have warned you about the lake," he roared. "Never mind. Get yourself cleaned up, and I'll get breakfast ready."

After much painful scrubbing with handfuls of grass, Littlenose was rid of the mud, although he still smelt a bit. He cheered up until Uncle Redhead produced the honeycomb and broke off a generous piece for him. "Good, eh?" he said as Littlenose forced himself to eat it. "Now you'll feel better."

Littlenose felt slightly sick.

The journey continued for the next few days, and Littlenose gradually learned to ignore his uncle's chatter. To his relief none of their overnight camps was near a suitable bathing place. But the supply of honey seemed endless, and Littlenose wondered how he could ever possibly have liked it.

It was exactly a week after leaving home that Uncle Redhead said, "Early to bed tonight. We've work to do tomorrow." What the work was he wouldn't say, but in the morning Littlenose was set to making a parcel of the flints which Uncle Redhead carried in his pack. Even Littlenose could see that these were the very best, top-quality flints, which were always difficult to come by.

After they left camp, they headed for a patch of forest. Then they paused on the edge of a clearing, and Littlenose's hair stood on end with fright. In front of them was a camp. It was quiet, and everyone seemed asleep. But it was not a Neanderthal camp. From the skin shelters slung between the trees, Littlenose knew that this was the camp of a tribe of Straightnoses. He was terrified, but Uncle Redhead led him around the edge of the clearing to a huge tree. Part way up the trunk was a hole, like an owl's nesting hole. Uncle Redhead reached into the hole and took out a small pouch. He replaced the pouch with the parcel of flints. Then, with a careful look around, he led the way back to their own camp.

Littlenose was still shaking with fright as they packed for the long journey home. But Uncle Redhead was as cheery as ever. "It's a good season," he said, as he looked at the coloured pebbles in the pouch.

"These people really know a good flint when they see one. I'm thinking of retiring soon."

"But that was a Straightnose camp!" said Littlenose.

"Of course," said his uncle. "They're good customers. Some of my best friends are Straightnoses. But they're a bit shy of us.

They think the Neanderthal folk are dangerous."

Littlenose could make nothing of all this. He felt they were lucky to have escaped in one piece.

The return journey was as bad as that coming. They marched for miles every day, most mornings started with a cold bath, and Uncle Redhead never stopped talking. There was honeycomb every day, and before they reached home Littlenose had toothache.

Two-Eyes trumpeted with joy when he saw Littlenose, and Mum cried and kissed him. Dad wasn't sure whether he was pleased or not.

As for Littlenose, he was so glad to be home that he wasn't bored again.

For almost a week, at least.

Bigfoot

One day, Dad told Littlenose that they were all going to spend a holiday with some of their relatives. Littlenose didn't want to go. And said so.

"You'll do as you're told for once," said Dad, "and like it."

"All right," said Littlenose, adding under his breath, "but I won't like it."

The real trouble was that even Dad

didn't think much of his sister's family whom they would be visiting. Most Neanderthal folk lived in tribes who made their homes in caves. During the Ice Age, life was very hard indeed, and neighbours who could help each other in times of trouble were essential. With water being drawn from the river, firewood being chopped, flints being chipped and all the bustle and activity of a Neanderthal living place going on from dawn to dusk, life was hectic. Which was how people liked it. Most of them, that is. For there were families who lived in remote places far from their nearest neighbours.

That was how Littlenose's Uncle Juniper and his family lived. Littlenose had never met them but he knew that their home was far away in the mountains where the juniper bushes grew. Juniper berries were prized as medicine by the Neanderthal doctors, and every autumn the people of the mountains brought the season's fruit down to market. Littlenose's uncle was one of the best known, which accounted for his name. This much Littlenose had been told, but he had heard much more while lying awake at night listening to Mum and Dad talking.

"How can anyone live like that?" said Dad. "They do nothing. They see nothing. A crowd of yokels. Hill-billies. You can't even get decent conversation out of them. When I met Juniper at the market last week he hardly said a word from first to last."

"He probably couldn't get a word in edgeways," said Mum. "And he did say enough to invite us all to stay. In any case, if you don't like them why did you accept?"

"I wasn't thinking," groaned Dad. "I thought they only wanted Littlenose."

Next morning, after breakfast, Mum began the task of sorting out what they would need on holiday. Littlenose laid out his spear, his fire-making flints and his lucky coloured stone, and said, "I'm ready." But to his disgust Mum made him pack several pairs of clean furs as well. Looking at the mound of baggage, Dad said, "I think we might have been quicker just wrapping up the whole cave. We *are* only going to be away for three weeks, not the rest of our lives."

It was just getting light when they loaded Two-Eyes and set off next day. Uncle Juniper's home was one week's march due east of their own cave, and Dad explained that if they walked with the rising sun in their faces and camped at evening with the setting sun at their backs they couldn't go wrong.

On the second day out, Dad decided that they weren't travelling fast enough and had better break camp much earlier the following day. He roused everyone while it was still pitch dark, and set off. As they stumbled through the gloom, Mum said,

"You're quite sure we're going the right way?"

"Am I in the habit of making mistakes?" said Dad.

Mum just sniffed, while Littlenose nodded silently.

Then the sun rose . . . far to the left.

Dad stopped and muttered something which nobody could make out, but which seemed to imply that the sun was in the wrong place. But they changed direction, and went on their way.

On the fourth day Dad said, "We'll soon meet Uncle Juniper. When we stop tomorrow evening the sun should set exactly between two peaks. We have to wait at the pass between the peaks for Juniper to guide us the rest of the way."

Next evening as they made camp

Littlenose watched the rim of the setting
sun slip down between two sharp mountain
tops. Before the light had completely gone
Dad scratched a mark on the ground like a
spear pointing towards the pass where
tomorrow they hoped to find Uncle Juniper.

In fact Uncle Juniper found *them* next
morning as they rested by a clear spring,
and they arrived at the Juniper family cave
before dusk.

It was very similar to the one in which

Littlenose lived, with one marvellous difference. His cousins had a cave of their own, a smaller one that opened off the family cave. Here he was tucked up for the night with the three other boys, but none of them wanted to sleep. They whispered together in the dark exchanging boy-news. Littlenose told them of his home by the big river, of his visits to the market and his hunting lessons. He told them of bears and hyenas and sabre-toothed tigers. His cousins listened with amazement to the long stories of all his adventures. Then he asked, "What do *you* do around here?"

After a long pause, one cousin said, "Throw stones."

After another, even longer, pause the second cousin said, "Gather berries."

After a pause that was so long that

Littlenose thought he had fallen asleep the third cousin said, "Throw more stones."

Littlenose's heart sank. This holiday was going to be every bit as dull as he imagined!

Next morning, after breakfast, Littlenose said, "What shall we do?" Without replying, his cousins stuck a row of sticks in the ground at the end of a stretch of green turf . . . and started to throw stones at them. They were very good at it, which Littlenose wasn't. They knocked the sticks flying every time, but Littlenose found that he could not even throw far enough, let alone straight and hard enough. Apart from the occasional squabble, they threw stones all that day. And the next. And the next. Littlenose was frantic with boredom, and his throwing arm ached. Then, he remembered the other thing his cousins did. "What about going berry picking?" he asked at lunch. His aunt looked up. "Yes," she said, "I could do with some blaeberries, but remember, don't go past the cairns." The cousins nodded. Littlenose didn't know what a cairn was, but he nodded too.

The berry picking was, if anything, more boring than the stone throwing. There were very few berries, and soon Littlenose's back ached from stooping. He straightened up, and saw a promising blaeberry patch some way off. He was going towards it when he heard a shout from the other boys: "Not past the cairn!" He waved and walked on, and they shouted again. Then he saw a huge heap of large stones, as tall as he was. Other heaps were in a long line across the hillside. These must be the cairns.

He shrugged and turned back. "Why?"
he asked. His cousins looked at each other
and mumbled something that sounded like
"bigfoot".

"Who's Bigfoot?" asked Littlenose. But
his cousins wouldn't explain and just
hurried back to the cave.

After supper, Dad took Littlenose to one
side and said, "I hope you haven't been
upsetting your cousins. The folk in these

parts are simple and superstitious. They say if you go past the line of stone cairns the local bogey man will grab you." Dad grinned. "He's tall, hairy, and you can smell him a long way off. And he leaves enormous footprints." Littlenose grinned back at Dad. It sounded very fanciful, but still the line of cairns was intriguing. He made up his mind to explore beyond them, if only to show his simple cousins that there was nothing to be afraid of.

Next morning, before anyone was awake, Littlenose crept from the cave and made his way to the blaeberry place. The early-morning mist made it difficult to see, and he groped his way carefully forward. Suddenly he stopped. A tall shape loomed in front of him and his hair stood on end with fright. But the figure didn't move.

Then the mist thinned in the breeze and he saw that it was one of the stone cairns. Sighing with relief, Littlenose pressed on.

The mist rolled away completely with the coming day, and he found himself crossing a steep, bare mountainside covered with stunted trees and scrubby bushes. Patches of last winter's snow lay here and there, and Littlenose was scanning the ground ahead when he noticed something odd about one of the patches. There were huge footprints on it. But they were old. The edges were blurred where the sun had melted the snow, and the more he looked at them the less sure he became that they *were* footprints. All the talk of Bigfoot was making his eyes play tricks on him. He went on his way.

Then he stopped at another snow patch.

Here there were more marks like the last.
But these were fresh, and most definitely
footprints. Something very big had passed
in front of him only a short time before!

For the second time, Littlenose's hair
stood on end. His mind went numb and he
couldn't think. He jumped at a sudden
sound. Something was coming out of the
bushes . . . In the split second before he

took to his heels, Littlenose had a glimpse of something tall, shaggy and man-shaped looming out of the dark undergrowth. Littlenose flew downhill over snow, rock and gravel. Behind him the thing shambled swiftly in pursuit, plodding rapidly on enormous feet and short, powerful legs. And it was gaining on him.

The giant creature took one stride for every three of Littlenose's. He knew that he could never outrun it, but if he could hide, Dad or Uncle Juniper would come looking for him. There was a dead tree straight ahead. It had been struck by lightning and stood white and bare against the dark green scrub. Littlenose ran the last few steps, and dragged himself up to safety.

From his branch Littlenose looked down on the creature. It was twice as tall as a man, covered with shaggy fur, and had small eyes and a wide mouth with jagged teeth. And there was a terrible smell – like dead animals and damp caves all jumbled together. There was no mistake – this was Bigfoot!

When Bigfoot reached the tree he grabbed the trunk and shook it hard, roaring with all his might. Littlenose shook like a leaf in a gale, while Bigfoot tried to climb after him. But the lower branches weren't strong enough and broke under his weight.

As he clung to the tree, Littlenose began to think. It might be a long time before anybody came to his rescue, and it seemed unlikely that the dead tree would stand much of Bigfoot's shaking. He had to do something before the whole lot crashed to

the ground. He rummaged furiously in his furs and fished out his fire-making flints. Animals were afraid of fire and Bigfoot was at least part animal. Quickly he struck a spark on to the dead leaves clinging to a withered branch. The leaves caught fire and the branch became a torch. Breaking it off, Littlenose leaned forward and carefully dropped the flaming branch. But Bigfoot sidestepped, and as the burning torch fell to the ground picked it up and threw it into the bushes.

"He's not all *that* animal," thought Littlenose in dismay. There seemed no point in lighting another branch, and he looked around in despair for a new idea. Then he realised that Bigfoot's attention had wandered. He was sniffing loudly, and swinging his head from side to side.

Littlenose saw that a grey pall of smoke was blowing across the hillside. The torch had set fire to the undergrowth. The smoke became thicker, and swirled around the foot of the tree until Bigfoot was only a dim, coughing shape. This was Littlenose's chance. He slithered to the ground, and under cover of the smoke ran as fast as he could. Behind him he heard thudding footsteps as Bigfoot took up the chase again. But now Littlenose could see the line of the cairns.

He passed the first cairn and glanced over his shoulder. Bigfoot was almost on him. Then he heard a voice: "Get down, Littlenose!" And at the same something whizzed past his ear. Littlenose threw himself flat and heard Bigfoot roaring angrily behind him. Raising his head he

saw a shower of well-aimed stones flying
through the air while Bigfoot tried to fend
them off with wildly waving arms.

At last the monstrous creature gave up and stumbled back up the mountainside and out of sight, leaving behind a trail of huge footprints and a dreadful smell. The cousins threw their remaining stones for luck before escorting Littlenose back to the cave.

The grown-ups weren't told of his adventure.

As he was leaving with Dad, Mum and Two-Eyes at the end of the holiday, Uncle Juniper said to Littlenose, "Well, and how would you like to live here with us in peace and quiet?"

"Actually," replied Littlenose, "I think the excitement would be too much for me. Goodbye, and thank you for having me."

Littlenose
the Joker

JOHN GRANT
Illustrations by Ross Collins

Contents

Littlenose the Joker

Littlenose was a boy in a Neanderthal tribe, and Neanderthal folk were quite a merry lot. Despite the cold of the Ice Age, the frequent lack of food and the danger from wild animals, they enjoyed a joke as much as anyone. They could be heard laughing and singing as they worked at chipping flints to make tools, or cut and sewed animal skins to make clothes. And one of the most fun-loving Neanderthal people was Littlenose.

While Littlenose and his family and friends were ready for a laugh at any time, there was one day in the year which they kept especially for playing tricks on each other. They called it Crocus Day. As soon as the first crocus appeared in bloom in the spring, then for that day anyone could play tricks on anyone else, the person playing the trick shouting, "CROCUS!" at the person tricked. As you might expect, it was one of Littlenose's favourite times of the year.

One spring day, Littlenose sat under his special tree where he did his more important thinking. Two-Eyes, his pet mammoth was with him, half asleep in the first warm weather since the previous autumn.

"I don't know what I'm going to do, Two-Eyes," said Littlenose. "Any day now the first crocus will be out, and I haven't thought of a single trick to play."

"If you ask me," thought Two-Eyes in his own mammoth way, "the whole idea is a piece of nonsense!" But, as usual, nobody asked him, and Littlenose went on: "I could tie a rope across the cave entrance to trip up Dad . . . but I did that last year! Or I could tie a long string to the tiger-skin rug, and pull it so that Mum would think it was alive . . . but I did that the year before!" He thought a while longer, then, as it was almost lunchtime, he went home.

After lunch, he still hadn't thought of a good Crocus joke, so he decided to look over his collection, in case an idea might just come to him.

Littlenose was a very enthusiastic collector. His collection contained dried leaves, stones with interesting marks on them, birds' feathers, snail shells, and a piece of broken antler. By evening he still hadn't had any ideas, but the collection in his corner of the cave was looking much tidier. He had almost forgotten Crocus Day, and he said to Two-Eyes, "Let's go collecting tomorrow. I've a feeling I'll be extra lucky, and find something special to collect."

Next morning after breakfast, he slung his hunting bag across his shoulder and set off with Two-Eyes. They went along by the river, up the hill and into the forest, and in no time at all Littlenose had collected quite a few interesting items: a bird's egg, a large dead beetle, and a piece of bark with markings that looked vaguely like a picture of Dad. So much for the forest, now for the open grassland. He'd found some of the best items in his collection there.

But not this time, it seemed. "Keep looking, Two-Eyes," said Littlenose. Two-Eyes gave a sort of mammoth "Hmph!" and turned his head this way and that as he wandered in a casual sort of fashion through the long grass and around the clumps of gorse which grew here and there.

Suddenly, he stopped. "What is it, Two-

Eyes?" said Littlenose. "Have you found something?"

Two-Eyes made not a sound, but stood stock still, his big ears spread to catch the faintest sound, and his trunk held out sniffing delicately at the breeze. Some way in front was a particularly large clump of gorse, and as Littlenose followed Two-Eyes' gaze, he thought he could just make out something. Something big was lurking in the bushes. And things which lurked in bushes were invariably dangerous. He couldn't actually see anything among the foliage, but he could see what had attracted Two-Eyes' attention. A large object was sticking out from among the leaves. It was a horn. Not an ordinary horn, but one which was quite extraordinary. It was *huge*. It was half as big as Littlenose.

"That can only be one thing, Two-Eyes,"
he said in a whisper. "A giant wild bull!"

But Two-Eyes was a mammoth, and
mammoths had much keener eyesight than
Neanderthal boys. He also remembered
what Littlenose had forgotten. The great
wild bulls lived deep in the forest, and it
would be most unlikely to find one out on
the open grassland. Also, giant bulls didn't
usually stay as still as this, particularly if
people were near. He decided to have a

closer look. "No, don't, Two-Eyes," said Littlenose, as the little mammoth walked boldly up to the bush, reached up with his trunk, and touched the horn. The horn dropped to the ground with a soft thump. One thing was certain. There was no wild giant bull on the other end!

Littlenose ran to join Two-Eyes. He examined the horn. It was old and discoloured. And the sharp tip had been broken off. But it seemed worth collecting. It might be useful for keeping things in. Littlenose lifted up the horn and looked inside. It was full of dirt and dust, and he tried to blow it out, but his hair and eyes got full of dust as it blew back in his face. So, he turned it round, put the broken tip to his mouth, and blew again. There was another great cloud of dust . . . then a loud bellowing sound!

Littlenose dropped the horn as if it were red-hot and jumped back, falling over a tuft of grass and sitting down with a thump. Two-Eyes was nowhere to be seen. Littlenose cautiously reached out to the horn and picked it up. Two-Eyes equally cautiously peered out from a distant clump of bushes. He walked slowly towards Littlenose and looked suspiciously at the horn. Timidly, he touched it with the tip of his trunk. Littlenose took a deep breath, and blew hard into the horn. The noise echoed across the landscape and set a flock of crows cawing in alarm at the edge of the forest. This time Two-Eyes ran only a short distance before he stopped and came back sheepishly towards Littlenose. And Littlenose now knew why Two-Eyes had been frightened. The sound from the horn was exactly like the bellow of an enraged woolly rhinoceros. He gave it a more gentle blow, and it sounded like a slightly annoyed woolly rhinoceros.

This was a treasure indeed! Littlenose said as much to Two-Eyes. Two-Eyes grunted in a resigned sort of fashion. He knew what was coming next. He was right. Littlenose heaved the horn across Two-Eyes' back where it balanced precariously, and they set off back home.

They were not far from the caves when they saw two figures ahead of them. It was

Nosey and one of the other men returning
empty-handed from a day's hunting.
Littlenose liked Nosey, and he was about to
shout and run after the men when he had a
brilliant idea. Did the horn *really* make a
sound like an enraged woolly rhinoceros?
Maybe he and Two-Eyes had imagined it.
They found a patch of long grass and hid.
Then Littlenose lifted the horn . . . and
BLEW!

It was wonderful! The two men dropped their spears and ran. "It's a woolly rhinoceros!" they heard Nosey yell. "ENRAGED! Run for your life."

Littlenose lay in the grass, and laughed and laughed until he was sore. Two-Eyes gave a sort of non-committal mammoth grunt. Actually, mammoths didn't have much of a sense of humour, and he thought the whole thing a bit ridiculous. When Littlenose had wiped the tears from his eyes, and peered over the top of the grass, Nosey and his friend had gone. "This is going to be fun," he said to Two-Eyes.

"This is going to lead to trouble," thought Two-Eyes. "As usual!"

The horn was much too big to join the rest of Littlenose's collection in his corner of the cave, so he hid it in a thicket near the edge of the woods. He would do something wonderful with it, but until he had decided what, it would be safe.

That day, Uncle Redhead was passing through the district, and dropped in for a visit. At supper, he said, "Spring's coming on fast. Any time now it'll be Crocus Day."

Crocus Day! Littlenose had completely forgotten. He had been so excited at finding the wonderful horn. And he still hadn't the faintest idea what tricks he would play. Uncle Redhead was in a reminiscent mood, and started to tell tales of Crocus Day tricks he had played when *he* was Littlenose's age. He had been the best joker in the district, throwing chestnuts into the fire so that they popped and sparked, startling everyone, or spreading bear grease on the stone floor at the entrance to the cave to make people slip and fall.

"Hmph!" said Mum. "It wasn't all *that* funny! I was the one who slipped!" She was, of course, Uncle Redhead's sister. But Littlenose thought it sounded hilarious. The snag was that it wasn't likely to come as a surprise to anyone after Uncle Redhead had been talking about it. He was really no nearer to thinking of a trick to play.

That is, until breakfast time the following morning. Neanderthal caves had no proper furniture, but handy rocks served just as well. Instead of a table, Littlenose ate his meals off a large flat rock, and smaller, round boulders, acted as seats. Littlenose was hungry, as usual, and he fidgeted as he waited impatiently for Mum to serve the food. As he fidgeted he was sure he felt his seat move. He wriggled, and sure enough the boulder rocked very slightly on the sandy floor of the cave. He was just going to tell Mum, when he had an idea. This might be the beginnings of a good joke. A Crocus Day trick that would be remembered for years . . . like Uncle Redhead's slippery floor. It would need a lot of preparation, and he couldn't start until he was sure of the right day.

Late that afternoon, Littlenose was playing in the woods with Two-Eyes when he saw something which made his heart leap. Among the long grass growing in a small clearing, he saw the dark spikes of crocus leaves. And among the crocus leaves were stalks with buds. And some of the buds were showing tips of colour. By tomorrow they would be crocus flowers in full bloom. Tomorrow would be Crocus Day.

Littlenose waited impatiently for the day to pass. Supper came and went. Then bedtime. Littlenose lay under the fur bed covers in his own special corner of the cave and worried. He was worried that the weather might suddenly turn cold or dull and the crocuses wouldn't open. And he was worried in case he fell asleep. The whole thing depended on staying awake until Mum and Dad were asleep. He had work to do. Hard work that had to be completed before getting up time.

At long last, apart from the occasional snore, silence fell on the caves of the Neanderthal folk. Littlenose slipped out of bed and tiptoed across the cave. The fire cast a warm glow of light, and a faint moonlight shone through the entrance.

Littlenose collected a handful of kindling and a flat piece of bone which he had hidden, and set to work. The sky outside was beginning to lighten with the coming day when he finished. He took a last look at his handiwork and went back to bed.

He had hardly closed his eyes, it seemed, when Mum was calling him. It was time to get up and fetch the water and the firewood. Rubbing his eyes, Littlenose got on with his morning chores, and it wasn't until he got back to the cave that he realised that Dad wasn't there. "Where's Dad?" he asked.

"Have you forgotten?" said Mum. "Dad has gone fishing with some friends. He left early. He won't be back until after breakfast. Breakfast isn't quite ready, so take your bedding out and give it a good shaking."

Bewildered, Littlenose dragged his fur

bedclothes out into the fresh air. His plan was going all wrong. It *depended* on Dad being at home for breakfast. He started shaking the dust and fluff out of the bedding. Suddenly, he gave a yell. "I've got something in my eye!"

"Let me look," said Mum. "Stay still! I can't see if you're jiggling about like that. Sit down." Still rubbing his eye, Littlenose followed her into the cave. "Here, where there's light to see," said Mum, and she pushed him down on the rock where Dad normally sat to eat. "Now, let's see . . ." Mum started to say. "Good gracious!"

Littlenose was lying flat on his back, and the rock seat had sunk out of sight into the sandy floor of the cave. Into the hole that had taken Littlenose half the night to dig! The pieces of stick holding the rock in

position had broken under his weight. But
it should have been *Dad* who collapsed,
when he sat down to breakfast. Then
Littlenose would have jumped up and
down shouting, "CROCUS!"

Mum said, "You're not hurt, are you?
Dad had better have a look at it when he
comes home. Let's see that eye of yours,
then we'll have breakfast."

Littlenose could have wept. What a start
to Crocus Day! He was sitting with Two-Eyes
under his favourite tree when he heard a
shout. People were hurrying from their
caves towards the river. From what they

said, Littlenose gathered that Dad and his friends had had extraordinary luck with their fishing, and the whole tribe was required to help carry home the catch. He might as well go along, too. Everyone was milling about among the high rocks along the river bank, their excited voices echoing loudly. Littlenose watched for a moment. Then a broad grin broke out on his face. He would play the biggest Crocus Day joke of all time. Involving the WHOLE TRIBE!

He raced to where the wild bull horn was hidden, and dragged it back towards the river and a handy patch of tall rushes. Then, puffing his cheeks out, he blew until he thought he would burst.

The bellowing sound blared out, echoing and re-echoing among the rocks. The people stopped in their tracks.

"A woolly rhinoceros!" cried one.

"ENRAGED!" cried another. And they ran and scrambled in all directions, falling over one another as the sound seemed to echo from everywhere at once.

"IT'S COMING OUT OF THE FOREST!"

"*Across the river!*"

"OVER THE HILL!"

And Littlenose lay among the rushes and laughed and laughed. He'd give them just one more for luck. Again the wild bellowing filled the air.

"It's getting closer," shouted someone. "Back to the caves!" Next moment it was a stampede.

"This is where I shout, 'CROCUS!'" thought Littlenose.

But as he opened his mouth, he realised

what had happened. The patch of rushes where he was hiding was between the river bank and the caves. Shouting in terror, the whole tribe raced for home, trampling through the rushes and everything else in their path, including Littlenose, who found himself flat on the ground under several dozen pairs of hard Neanderthal feet.

As the sound of the retreat faded in the

distance, Littlenose picked himself up, spitting out mud and pieces of rush.

"CROCUS . . . everybody!" he said, as he felt his bruises.

Two-Eyes appeared, wearing a very I-told-you-so look. Littlenose looked around for the horn. It was in a million pieces. "Come to think of it, Two-Eyes," he said as they set off home, "Crocus Day *is* a pretty silly idea anyway."

His immediate problem was to think of a good story for Dad regarding the mysterious behaviour of his rock seat.

And, in any case, it was another whole year before he would have to think of a Crocus Day joke.

Squeaky

Littlenose was one of the very few of the Neanderthal folk who kept a pet. He had Two-Eyes, the baby mammoth, and was very fond of him indeed. Yet, as Two-Eyes had found out very early on, being Littlenose's pet was hard work. Littlenose loved to play games with Two-Eyes, but he also loved to play tricks on him, and not very pleasant ones at that. The latest had

been when Dad had gone to look for gulls'
eggs in the marshes. Littlenose and Two-Eyes
went with him to help. However, as their
idea of helping was to run in all directions
at once, falling over tussocks, each other
and Dad, they were soon told to go away
and sit quietly.

Two-Eyes promptly lay down and fell
asleep, but Littlenose was bored. He started
to make a flower chain with marsh
marigolds, but it broke, and he threw it
down in disgust. Then he tried skimming
stones on a pool, until one of them just
missed Dad, who shook his fist at Littlenose.
Then Littlenose had a wonderful idea, and
he laughed just thinking about it.

He began picking the soft, fluffy heads
off the cotton grass. Then he tiptoed back
to Two-Eyes, who was still asleep, and

began to stick them on to the little mammoth's black fur. Two-Eyes didn't wake, and Littlenose gathered more and more of the white tufts and stuck them on until not a hair of black fur could be seen. Two-Eyes was completely white. The real fun came, of course, when Two-Eyes woke.

Mammoths were very fussy creatures, forever preening their fur with their trunks, and Two-Eyes went quite mad when he found himself covered in cotton grass. He trumpeted and squealed, and he ran around pulling the white fluff off with his trunk. Then he saw Littlenose standing laughing. This was too much. He put down his head and butted Littlenose, who sat down with a thump, but didn't stop laughing until Two-Eyes had disappeared in the direction of home.

When he got home later with Dad, Littlenose was not really surprised to find that Two-Eyes was nowhere to be found. When Littlenose and his tricks became too much for him, Two-Eyes would sometimes go off to visit some wild mammoth friends for a week or two.

But, as the weeks became a month, then two months, Littlenose missed Two-Eyes very much. He became quite downhearted, and even the arrival of Uncle Redhead on a short visit didn't cheer him up much. In fact, he felt even *worse* because Uncle Redhead seemed to talk about nothing but pets. "There was this friend of mine," he said. "He had a pet lion. Bought it from a man for twenty red pebbles."

"Was it tame?" asked Mum.

"That's what my friend asked," said Uncle Redhead. "And the man he bought if from said, 'Sure, it'll eat off your hand'."

"Did it?" asked Littlenose.

"No," said Uncle Redhead, "it ate off his leg!" And he went into gales of laughter at his own joke.

Uncle Redhead left next morning. He shook Littlenose by the hand and said, "Goodbye and good luck," and gave him an apple. He didn't feel like an apple just

then, so he put it carefully among his
things in his own special corner of the cave.

When he did decide to eat his apple he
had a surprise. There were small teeth
marks on it. "Who's been eating my
apple?" he thought. He wasn't long in
finding out. He heard a scuffle and a
squeak, and lifting up his
fur hunting robe he
saw a very small
mouse crouched in
a corner. It
squeaked again
and watched
Littlenose with
black, beady eyes.
Littlenose stared
back. It was a handsome little animal, with
a glossy coat and a long tail. And it didn't

seem all that afraid, for it stood up on its hind legs suddenly and squeaked even louder than before.

"I think it wants the apple," said Littlenose under his breath. And he bit off a small piece and carefully held it out. Just as carefully the mouse edged forward and took a gentle nibble before darting back to its corner. Littlenose laid the piece of apple beside it. "Here you are, Squeaky," he said. "You can be my new pet."

Littlenose played happily with Squeaky, who was very tame, until he heard Mum calling him for supper. Picking Squeaky up carefully, he took his place while Mum served the meal. Dad hadn't come in yet, and Mum was just filling a clay bowl with stewed rhinoceros, when she gave a terrible scream and leapt up on the large boulder, which served as a table. Littlenose jumped up in alarm, while Mum shrieked, "Get it out! Get that horrible brute out of here!"

Her cries brought Dad at a run. "What is it?" he shouted. "A bear? Sabre-toothed tiger?"

"A MOUSE!" cried Mum. "There!" And she pointed to where Littlenose stood, still holding Squeaky.

"It's Squeaky," said Littlenose, "look!" And he held Squeaky out for Mum to have a better look. But Mum didn't want a better look. She lifted the bowl of stewed rhinoceros above her head and cried, "Come one step closer . . ." She didn't need to say any more. Dad grabbed Littlenose by the scruff of the neck and ran him out of the cave. "Don't come back until you've got rid of it," he said, and trying to keep his face straight he went back in to comfort Mum.

"What on earth am I to do?" thought Littlenose. "I can't just leave Squeaky outside by himself. He might get eaten or stood on." Then he remembered his secret pocket. Neanderthal boys didn't as a rule have pockets, but Uncle Redhead had once shown Littlenose how to fashion one in his furs. Now Littlenose carefully tucked Squeaky into his pocket, where he curled up happily and promptly fell asleep.

Dad looked up as Littlenose came back to the cave. "Have you taken care of the mouse?" he asked.

"Yes," said Littlenose, quite truthfully, then sat down and got on with his supper. For a time there was silence except for the crunchings, slurpings and gurglings normal to a Neanderthal meal. Then Mum said sharply, "Stop fidgeting, Littlenose, for goodness' sake." Littlenose gave a sickly smile and sat still for a moment, but he was finding it more and more difficult.

Squeaky, after a short but refreshing nap in Littlenose's pocket, had decided to explore. Making his way through a mouse-sized hole in the pocket he was wriggling his way inside Littlenose's furs. His tiny claws scratched, and his tail and whiskers tickled, making it agony for Littlenose to sit still.

"What's the matter now?" said Mum, as Littlenose stopped eating and sat with hunched shoulders and screwed-up eyes. Before he could answer, Mum leapt up, scattering food in all directions and shouting, "There it is again!"

Squeaky had at length worked his way

right up inside Littlenose's furs, popped out at his neck, then leapt down to his supper. Littlenose didn't wait to be told this time. He grabbed Squeaky and fled, while Mum had hysterics and Dad shouted after him.

Littlenose made his way to his favourite tree, and sat down with Squeaky on his knee. "Much as I like you, Squeaky," he said, "as a pet you're not much of a success. Two-Eyes at least got me out of trouble from time to time, but all you seem to be able to do is get me into it." Squeaky said nothing, but Littlenose thought that he looked a bit sorry for all the upset he had caused. One thing was certain, squeaky could not return to the cave. Littlenose would have to find somewhere safe for him. He found an old,

cracked clay pot, into which he put
Squeaky with some berries for his supper.
Then he tucked it into a space among the
roots of the tree for safety. He said goodnight,
then went home to bed, hoping things
might have calmed down a bit by then.

By next morning, Littlenose had made
up his mind. He retrieved Squeaky from
the old pot and spoke to him very seriously.
"We are going to find Two-Eyes," he said.
"It's high time he came home. For one
thing, he knows how to behave as a pet
should, and can give you a few tips. For
another, you'll like him, although he is just
a bit bigger." Then he put Squeaky carefully
into his pocket.

Littlenose had thought that finding
Two-Eyes would be easy. He climbed a
high hill and gazed across the land hoping

to spot a lively mammoth herd, but nothing was moving as far as the eye could see. Then he tried looking for tracks. One thing about mammoth herds was that they left roads rather than tracks. As they moved from place to place they crushed the grass, flattened the bushes and trampled even small trees with their great feet. Even a single mammoth made footprints like no other animal. Yet Littlenose hunted high and low all morning without seeing as much as a crushed leaf or a single footprint. At midday he had decided to give up and go home, and was already on his way when he stopped and looked at the ground. The earth was sandy, and pressed into it was an unmistakable footprint. A mammoth footprint!

"It's Two-Eyes'. I know it is," he shouted

out loud. And he took Squeaky out of his pocket to have a look. "Maybe he's already on his way home," he went on, completely ignoring the fact that Two-Eyes was a baby mammoth and made fairly small footprints. This was huge!

But minor details like that rarely bothered Littlenose. He scouted around for more footprints and quickly found another. Then another. He could now make out a whole line stretching into the distance. All he had to do was follow them, and there at the end of the trail would be Two-Eyes!

And a very long trail it turned out to be.

He even lost it at one point where it left
the soft ground and crossed bare rock. He
picked it up again at the edge of the forest,
where it was so clear that he raced along
with his eyes on the ground, not looking
where he was going. Where he was going
was right into a clump of bushes that had
been chosen by a black bear for a quiet
nap. It was just dozing off when the sky fell
on its head. At least, that's what it thought.

Littlenose had blundered right over the bear and sat down hard on its head. The bear quickly leapt up, but Littlenose was quicker and was soon high in the branches of a tree, while Squeaky clung to a twig beside him. The bear stood on its hind legs, its head swaying from side to side as it tried to discover what had disturbed it. After muttering and grumbling to itself, it ambled away into the forest.

Waiting until the sounds of the bear had died in the distance, Littlenose scrambled to the ground. Then, with Squeaky safely back in his pocket, he hurried along the mammoth trail. It left the forest and began to cross the bare heath. Littlenose was by now very weary. The footprints led to a brownish-coloured hummock by a pile of boulders, and Littlenose made up his mind that he would sit down and rest there.

But halfway, he stopped in amazement. The hummock was growing. Higher and higher it rose, and he saw that what he thought had been brown grass or bracken was fur! The hummock was now standing on four mighty legs. Could it be . . .?

A glimpse of long curved tusks and a trunk told him that it could. It was a mammoth he had been trailing all right, but a very large grown-up one, not with a herd. Then he remembered his father speaking about rogue mammoths. They lived alone, and were more bad-tempered than anything you could imagine. The creature was half-turned away from Littlenose, and he hoped that it might go on its way without seeing him. Then it wheeled round, spread its ears and gave an almighty roar as it raised its trunk

in the air. Littlenose didn't wait to see what
it would do next. He ran.

Almost immediately he felt the ground
shake beneath him. The rogue mammoth
was in hot pursuit. Its long legs ate up the
distance between them. Its eyes were red

and angry, and firmly fixed on the fleeing figure of Littlenose, while the sharp points of its tusks pointed straight at him. Littlenose glanced over his shoulder, and in that instant he tripped and fell. The roaring of the mammoth grew deafening.

And then there was a moment of awful silence.

Littlenose saw that the mammoth was no longer looking at him. It was gazing at something in the grass. Then it took a step backwards. It was shaking with fright, and instead of roaring, it squealed and whimpered, then turned in its tracks and ran. In no time at all it was out of sight. But what terrible thing had frightened a rogue mammoth? "Squeaky!" cried Littlenose. "I didn't know that mammoths were afraid of mice. I thought it was only

Mum." And he sat Squeaky on his shoulder and set off in the direction of home.

And who should be waiting for him when he got there but Two-Eyes. Littlenose threw his arms around the little mammoth. "How I've missed you, Two-Eyes!" he cried. "But you must meet your new friend, Squeaky." But Squeaky was nowhere to be found. Life as Littlenose's pet had proved just a bit wearing, and he had gone on his way.

Littlenose's cousins

Littlenose heard Dad shouting long before he reached the cave. There was nothing new in Dad's shouting, but this sounded different. "Probably something I've done," thought Littlenose, and he crept towards the cave entrance, trying to catch what Dad was shouting about.

"But it's only a one-apartment cave," Dad shouted again. "How can it possibly hold eight people? Why did you invite them in the first place?"

"We owe them a visit," came Mum's voice. "They were very hospitable when we visited them in the mountains. It's the least we can do."

Now Littlenose understood. His Uncle Juniper and his whole family were coming to stay. Uncle Juniper lived many days' journey away in the high mountains, where he gathered the berries of the juniper bushes for a living. Juniper berries were highly prized by the Neanderthal folk for making medicine, and every autumn Uncle Juniper came down from the mountains to sell his fruit at the market. He was really very famous, but because he lived so far away, very few people had actually met him.

Mum spoke again. "Nosey's wife told me

that her husband had met Juniper at the market, and that he had his whole family with him. So I sent a message asking them to stay for a few days."

Littlenose recalled his holiday in the mountains. Uncle Juniper had three boys who were, of course, Littlenose's cousins. But then, the Juniper family lived in a spacious two-apartment cave with plenty of room for visitors. Litttlenose began to understand why Dad had been shouting. The Junipers lived by themselves, with no neighbours nearer than the other side of the mountains. They were simple people, and Dad unkindly called them Country Bumpkins, Hillbillies and Yokels. Still, it would mean someone new to play with, and Littlenose began to look forward to his cousins' arrival.

The Juniper family arrived late on the afternoon a few days later. Littlenose shook hands with his Uncle, kissed his Aunt and turned to greet the boys.

"Hi, there, Littlenose," said the biggest cousin, giving Littlenose a rather too hearty thump on the back. "How does a mammoth get down from an oak tree?"

"Eh?" said Littlenose, still trying to get his breath.

"Sits on a leaf and waits for autumn," said the cousin. And the three of them shrieked with laughter, nudging each other and Littlenose and generally falling about.

"I suppose that's meant to be funny," thought Littlenose.

It was the same during the evening meal. The grown-ups were so busy talking among themselves that they paid no attention to the boys, and Littlenose found it difficult to get on with the important business of eating. First one, then another of the Juniper boys nudged him and whispered things like: "Why do mammoths never forget? Because no one ever tells them anything!" and, "What do you call a deaf mammoth? Anything you like; it can't hear you!"

Littlenose tried to edge away out of earshot, then Mum looked up and said, "For goodness sake, sit still and don't fidget. Look at your cousins! They're behaving themselves!"

At last it was bedtime, and Littlenose hoped that a good night's sleep might help things. But not a bit of it. The cousins giggled and whispered in the dark more of their stupid mammoth jokes, and when Littlenose said, "Please be quiet and let me get some sleep," Dad shouted, "Be quiet, Littlenose; you'll wake your cousins." It was all very unfair!

At breakfast, Littlenose decided that the best thing was to ignore the Juniper boys, even when they leaned right over and whispered in his ear, "How do mammoths catch squirrels?" He just looked straight in front and waited for Mum to serve breakfast.

"Don't be so rude to your guests, Littlenose," said Dad. "Answer them when they speak to you."

Littlenose sighed at the great injustice of

it all, but decided to say nothing, and had just started to eat when the smallest cousin said, "Look, Littlenose! Over there."

Heeding Dad's words, Littlenose looked, but could see nothing remarkable.

"Oh, it's gone," said the cousin, and Littlenose went back to his breakfast. It seemed to have an odd flavour, but he was hungry and tucked in just the same. The cousins were eating more slowly, and seemed more interested in watching him than in eating. The taste grew stronger the farther he got down his clay bowl. And when he reached the dead frog at the bottom he knew why. He also knew who had put it there. But before he could do anything about it, Mum chased the boys outside to play while she cleared up.

Two-Eyes, who had been made to sleep outside to make room for the visitors, came running up to Littlenose. Jumping on the little mammoth's back, Littlenose said, "Come on, Two-Eyes, let's go somewhere for a quiet think." And leaving his Juniper cousins to their own devices, they galloped away into the woods.

The first quiet thought that Littlenose had was to run away from home, at least until the visitors had gone. But his second thought was that it would be much easier to keep out of their way as much as possible. Having made up his mind, he went back to the caves. A lady called from one of them, "Hello, Littlenose. How are you today?"

"Fine, thank you," said Littlenose.

He was about to strike up a conversation when the lady stooped down and said, "I wonder who could have left this?" A large skin-wrapped parcel was lying by the cave entrance. She was just about to pick it up when the parcel gave a leap and bounced along the ground to disappear into a clump of bushes. At the last moment Littlenose saw the string and heard an unmistakable giggle. The lady had sat down with a thump and was shrieking her head off. People came running from the other caves. "It's that terrible boy," she cried, pointing at Littlenose. "Playing tricks like that! It shouldn't be allowed! It isn't good for people, that sort of thing!"

Littlenose tried to explain, but no one would listen. The cousins, meanwhile,

stood at the back of the crowd, grinning all over their faces.

Littlenose arrived home to a stern talk from Dad on the subject of annoying the neighbours. It was made even worse by Dad's insisting on referring to the cousins as perfect examples of Neanderthal boyhood. The evening meal was a repeat of the previous one, except that the supply of

mammoth jokes had apparently run out
and the cousins kept up a running stream of
equally unfunny jokes about sabre-tooth tigers.

At last it was bedtime. With eight people
it was a bit of a squash in the cave, but
Littlenose had managed to keep his fur bed
covers just a bit separate from the others.
With a sigh of relief at the end of a pretty
miserable day, he slid down beneath the
covers. Next moment he was leaping
around holding his foot and yelling at the
top of his voice. "Something bit me!"

Everyone came running, Dad pulled back
the bedclothes . . . and the
angry-looking hedgehog
which had been
trying to find a
way out since
the cousins had put

it in earlier, scuttled into a corner and rolled into a ball. Dad was furious. "You know the rules about pets," he shouted. "You're lucky I let Two-Eyes into the cave. Now, get that creature out at once." But the creature, guessing that it was not exactly welcome, and needing some fresh air anyway, had unrolled and vanished into the night.

Littlenose lay awake that night wishing he had decided to leave home after all. After breakfast next morning he went off and sat under his favourite tree, where he did most of his important thinking. He was quite alone, having managed to give the cousins the slip, while Two-Eyes had gone off on some business of his own. Littlenose considered all sorts of attractive schemes for getting his own back.

For instance, he knew of a cave in the forest which was the home of a particularly evil-tempered black bear. Supposing he could trick his cousins into thinking that there was some special treat in the cave! There would be for the bear! Perhaps he might lure them on to a floating log in the river and send them sailing all the way to the sea? Oh, dear, why did all the best ideas have to be the most difficult to put into practice? His daydreams were shattered by a sudden noise. Sudden noises usually spelled danger in those days, and Littlenose was about to take to his heels when he recognised something in the noise. It was a squeal, like that given by a small and frightened mammoth. Littlenose jumped to his feet. The squealing was coming closer, but it was accompanied by a strange jangling and clattering. The bushes parted, and Two-Eyes burst through, his eyes wide with terror. He was desperately trying to get away from a clattering collection of broken pots and old bones which came bouncing out of the bushes behind him, attached by a long string to his tail. There was no need to ask who had put them there. Two-Eyes ran to Littlenose, and in a moment the string was untied and the little mammoth sank breathless to the grass.

This was going too far! Playing tricks on Littlenose and even Neanderthal ladies was one thing, but to frighten a poor harmless creature like Two-Eyes was too much. Littlenose, of course, conveniently forgot that he spent more time playing tricks on Two-Eyes than anything else. He would have his revenge if it was the last thing he did.

And strangely, that very afternoon he got the inklings of a plan.

When Littlenose and Two-Eyes returned to the cave they found that the Juniper boys were still out, but that the grown-ups were sitting around the fire talking. Dad was saying, "Yes, the Old Man, the leader of our tribe, is anxious to meet you. He's asked me to invite you on his behalf to a reception tomorrow. I'll warn you now, he fancies himself at making speeches and you're likely to be bored to tears. But he usually lays on a good spread at these sorts of things."

"What about the boys?" asked Uncle Juniper.

"Oh, they can come in time for the food," said Dad. "We'll leave Littlenose with them. He knows where the place is."

Littlenose sat in his own special corner of the cave and hugged himself with delight. If he could work things right, he would have a magnificent revenge for himself, Two-Eyes and the neighbour lady. That evening, he sat with his cousins outside the cave chatting about this and that, and listening to more terrible jokes. During a lull in the conversation, he looked up and said with a sigh, "Well, I'm certainly glad it isn't me."

"What do you mean?" asked the oldest cousin.

"Surely they've told you," said Littlenose. "You've been chosen to be presented to the Old Man."

"What of it?" said the cousin.

"Ah, now I understand," said Littlenose. "They probably didn't want to worry you. I don't blame them. People have been known to run away from home to avoid being presented. I was scared stiff, I don't mind telling you, when it was my turn. That was when the Old Man gave me my special spear." Littlenose neglected to say that the presentation of the spear had been the result of a considerable misunderstanding, but that's another story.

The cousins were leaning forward now, eager to hear more. And Littlenose didn't disappoint them. "Listen carefully," he said. "This is very important." And Littlenose told them such a convincing story that by the time he had finished even he was almost believing it.

"The Old Man," he said, "is leader of the tribe, and to be presented to him is a great honour. But it isn't easy. Leaders of tribes aren't like ordinary men. That's why they're leaders. They are proud and fierce, with strange powers. Why, it's said that the Old Man can stop a charging rhinoceros with one glance. It's his eyes, you see, which are to be feared. No one has ever looked him straight in the eye and lived to tell of it! You will be presented to the Old Man tomorrow in the presence of the whole tribe; and because I have already done it, I have

been entrusted with seeing that you get everything right. Because, if you don't . . ." Littlenose paused dramatically, and the cousins sat with mouths open in wonder. "No wonder," thought Littlenose, "that Dad calls them 'simple country folk'."

Before setting out for the Old Man's reception the next day, Dad took Littlenose to one side. "You'd only be bored with the grown-up chat," he said. "Bring the boys when the shadow reaches the pebble." And he stuck a twig in the ground so that it cast a long shadow in the sunlight, and placed a pebble a little way ahead of the shadow.

As soon as the grown-ups had gone, Littlenose turned to his cousins and said, "Right. Time to get ready! Remember what I said about the mud. It's to show that you are truly humble in the presence of the

Old Man. And don't forget how you approach him. On no account must you look directly at his face." The three cousins disappeared outside, and Littlenose quickly moved the pebble a little farther from the twig's shadow. The cousins returned and started smearing handfuls of mud on themselves. A ring round each eye. Patches on each cheek. A dab on the nose. And rings and dots on arms, legs and bodies. Littlenose could hardly believe that they were actually doing it. The shadow had reached the spot which Dad had marked with the pebble. "I must go on ahead, now," said Littlenose. "Follow me when the shadow reaches the pebble."

The grown-ups were gathered in the sunshine outside the Old Man's cave when Littlenose came wandering up looking very downcast. "Where are the boys?" asked Uncle Juniper.

"Oh, they're messing about with mud and stuff," said Littlenose.

At that moment, a gasp went up from the assembled guests as three strange figures appeared. They were crawling on their hands and knees . . . backwards. Slowly they approached the Old Man, who said, "Well, bless my soul! What funny people." Someone tittered. "Stand up and let me see you," said the Old Man. They stood up, but with eyes shut tight, and the laughter grew at the weird spectacle of three boys covered in splodges of mud, eyes shut, and trembling with terror. Uncle Juniper wasn't laughing, however. "One of your local customs?" said the Old Man, turning to him.

Instead of replying, Uncle Juniper
grabbed at the boys, and cuffed their ears,
while they yelled, "But we thought . . ."
And the whole tribe laughed and laughed,
but no one laughed louder than Littlenose

- unless it was the lady neighbour.

That was the end of the visit. With the boys gone, Littlenose relaxed again, and was soon happily playing tricks on Two-Eyes as was, after all, only proper.

The Fox Fur Robe

It was a crisp Ice Age autumn day. The Neanderthal folk were busy with preparations for another Ice Age winter, collecting firewood, gathering wild fruit and nuts, and looking over their winter furs. The men of the tribe were mainly occupied with checking their winter hunting equipment. They made sure that every fire-making flint sparked properly . . . and they spread out their hunting robes in the sun to air.

Littlenose spread his out on a flat rock close to the cave, and stood back to admire it. It was one of his proudest possessions, and he explained to Two Eyes: "Mum made my hunting robe for me. She hadn't enough of any one fur, so it's really a bit of everything. Bear, squirrel, rabbit, wolf. And fox . . . with a tail. It's the only hunting robe in the tribe with a tail. Probably the only one in the whole world." Two-Eyes tried to look interested. He had his own fur coat and didn't need a robe, and he hid a mammoth yawn behind his trunk as Littlenose chattered on.

Dad came out of the cave with his hunting robe over one arm. He shook out the dust and carefully put it on, the hood

over his head. Mum came out of the cave
after him.

"You're not wearing that terrible old
thing, are you?" she asked.

"What's wrong with it?" said Dad.

"It's ragged, and torn, and worn. And it's
full of holes," said Mum.

"But, apart from that?" said Dad.

"It's a perfect disgrace," said Mum, going

back into the cave. "To the family . . . and to the whole tribe!"

"What do you mean, 'disgrace'?" shouted Dad after her. "I'm the best hunter."

"And the worst dressed!" echoed Mum's voice from inside, followed by a loud rattling of cooking pots bringing the conversation to an end.

Dad went off by himself, muttering, "Disgrace, indeed!" And Littlenose turned back to his own hunting robe, which was in very good condition.

Over the evening meal, Dad sat, brooding. He wouldn't admit it, but Mum was right. There was a market in a week's time, the last before the Ice Age winter closed in and made travelling even more difficult than normal. He might just pick up an end-of-season bargain. He cleared his throat.

"Thinking of going to the market," he said casually. "Anything you need?"

Mum smiled quietly to herself. "There's the odd thing I could do with. Bone needles. A new bone ladle."

"Right," said Dad. "I'll take Littlenose and Two-Eyes. It's time that Littlenose learned something about trading. He could do worse than watch me in action. When it comes to driving a hard bargain—"

"Yes, we know," said Mum. "And Two-Eyes can help carry all your hard bargains home."

When market day came, Dad hauled Littlenose out of bed while it was still dark. The sun was only just coming over the hills when they left the caves behind. Littlenose had visited the market several times, and the way never seemed to get any shorter. As usual it was noon before they reached the circle of trees on the hill where the Neanderthal folk gathered to trade and exchange furs, flints, spears, axes, food, drink, and gossip.

After a quick snack, Dad started a tour of the various traders, while Littlenose trailed behind him and Two-Eyes took himself off to a sheltered spot for a nap. They passed several men selling household articles like bone needles and ladles, but Dad's mind seemed to be on other things. At last, they stopped at the foot of a tall tree where an old man sat cross-legged beside a great heap of furs. "Now," said Dad to Littlenose, "watch closely. The first rule is never to appear too eager to buy! Haggle about the price. That's the secret to driving a hard bargain."

"Can I help you?" said the old man.

"Thank you," said Dad. "Just browsing."
And he began to rummage among a heap
of black bear-skin hunting robes.

The old man beckoned to Littlenose.
"You seem a fine young fellow. A credit to
your noble father, I'm sure." And he handed
him an apple. Littlenose said, "Thank
you," and took the apple. "Yes, I said to
myself," said the old man to no one in
particular, "a person of distinction. A chief
at the very least. Am I right?"

". . . er, not exactly," said Dad.

"Not at all," thought Littlenose.

"A person of breeding. And taste. Very
rare these days, and a joy to behold . . .
and serve. Allow me, sir." The old man
stood up and took Dad's arm, and guided
him over to another pile of furs partly
hidden by the tree. "A more exclusive

selection," said the old man. "For those who really know about such things."

Littlenose watched in astonishment. Dad, his eyes alight, was holding the fur robes up one after the other. These were none of your common black bear or grey wolf. They were snowy white, gold and brown striped, yellow with brown spots. Dad was almost drooling with excitement as he hauled out from the foot of the pile a hunting robe, the likes of which Littlenose had never seen before. It was an exquisite creation in fully-fashioned red fox fur. Or, at least, that's how the old man described it, as he slipped it on to Dad's shoulders and stood back.

"How much?" said Dad, hoarsely.

The old man shook his head. "It's not for sale. It's made to measure for a high

chief of the Mountain People. To be
collected today. Sorry."

Dad just stood as the old man took the
red fox fur robe, folded it carefully and
placed it on top of the heap. Littlenose
thought this was strange - why wasn't
something to be collected today on top of
the pile already?

"Another time, perhaps," the old man

was saying as Dad walked away with a very strange look.

"What about the haggling and the hard bargain bit?" thought Littlenose.

For the rest of the afternoon Dad wandered about looking at the various things for sale. He bought a bundle of bone needles and a ladle, but nothing else from the list which Mum had given him, while Littlenose looked for something to buy with the five white pebbles he had earned doing odd jobs for the neighbours.

At length, as the sun slipped lower in the sky, they found themselves back by the tree where the old man sat with his furs. He called over to Dad. "This is indeed your lucky day, your lordship. I've just had some very sad news. The high chief of the Mountain People was eaten this afternoon.

By a sabre-tooth tiger."

"You mean . . .?" said Dad.

"Yes," said the old man. "The red fox fur robe will go to waste unless, that is, someone of good taste and—"

"I'll take it!" shouted Dad. "How much do you want?"

"Now," thought Littlenose, "is where we see some real hard bargaining." But, to his astonishment, when the old man said, "Twenty green pebbles," Dad didn't even pause as he went on " . . . and I'm giving it away. Taking the food out of the mouths of my wife and children . . ."

Dad was already pouring his coloured pebbles out of their leather pouch and desperately counting them. Red ones, green ones, a few yellow, and a handful of white. He muttered to himself, counting on his fingers, then he turned to Littlenose.

"I'm five white pebbles short. Have you any?" Littlenose hesitated for a moment, then handed Dad his pebbles.

With shaking hands, Dad thrust two handfuls of pebbles at the old man and snatched up the red fox fur robe. "A pleasure to do business with you, sir," said the old man.

"I bet it is," thought Littlenose.

Two-Eyes was surprised not to be laden down with a pile of Dad's purchases. But Mum was even more surprised when they arrived home. It was dark, and Mum was busy at the back of the cave. She saw the figure in the red fox fur robe in the light from the fire and hurried forward. "I'm afraid my husband isn't home yet, sir—" she started to say, then stopped. "Good gracious! It's YOU!" she cried, and sat down with a thump.

Littlenose came into the cave. "It's Dad's new hunting robe," he said. "Fox fur. Fully-fashioned."

Mum was too astonished to say any more. Dad gave her the needles and bone ladle, then, being careful to avoid making creases, he sat down to wait for Mum to bring supper.

It was late, and they went to bed as soon as they had eaten, Dad very reluctantly taking off his new robe.

When Littlenose woke next morning, Dad had already gone out. He came in just as they were sitting down for breakfast . . .

and he was wearing the fox fur hunting robe. "Just been for a stroll," he said. "Air's marvellously fresh this time of the morning." He sat down, and Mum began ladling out his breakfast. A tiny drop splashed out of the clay bowl. Dad cringed back. "Careful!" he shouted. "Don't throw it about like that! It's everywhere!" And he rubbed and scrubbed at an invisible spot of breakfast on the red fur.

After breakfast, Littlenose prepared to go out to play with Two-Eyes. The weather had turned mild, and Mum said to Littlenose, "I don't think you need wear your winter furs." Dad had to go to see Nosey the tracker on a matter of business, and Mum watched in amazement as he settled the new robe neatly on his shoulders and smoothed the fur with his hands before going out into the warm sun.

Long before Dad reached Nosey's cave, Nosey saw a large crowd approaching. In front was Dad, pretending not to notice the other hunters who pointed at the red fox fur robe and shouted things like: "It's the new autumn fashion! Red fox? Red face, you mean!" And the man was right. Dad was boiling under his hunting robe, and his face glowed crimson. But he tried to ignore his discomfort, as he ignored the remarks.

"I'll take your robe," said Nosey, as Dad entered the cave.

"No, no. It's quite all right," said Dad hastily. "I'm not stopping more than a few moments."

"Please yourself," said Nosey, as Dad sat down and surreptitiously wiped his brow with the back of his hand. The business, about the last hunt before the winter, was settled quickly.

During the week before the hunt, Dad was hardly to be seen without his red fox fur hunting robe, and after a time people got used to it and stopped making humorous remarks.

On the day of the hunt the men of the tribe gathered at dawn in front of the caves. By this time the weather had turned definitely wintry, and they all wore their hunting robes. They were made from brown bear, grey wolf, and only one was red fox! If nothing else, Dad was conspicuous!

The hunting party set off, led as usual by Nosey and his incredibly sensitive nose. Through the forest they went in single file, the apprentice hunters (including

Littlenose) bringing up the rear. Then Nosey held up his hand and the hunters halted, while Nosey crouched low and sniffed and snuffled among the pine needles. He stood up, pointed, and whispered, "There, thirty . . . no, I tell a lie . . . twenty-nine paces away is a bull elk."

That was good news. There was enough meat on a bull elk to feed the tribe for several weeks. The hunting party began to circle around through the trees to get downwind of the elk, their hunting robes making them almost invisible as they merged with the shadows beneath the trees. Well, almost! Everybody merged . . . except Dad. The red fox fur of his hunting robe positively shone out, and Nosey signalled with his hand for Dad to get back behind a tree trunk. But it was too late.

The elk came grazing its way into the clearing where the Neanderthal hunters waited, hidden amidst the gloom of the forest. Then it stopped. What was that? Something man-sized and bright red. The bull elk hadn't got where it was by hanging around asking questions . . . even of itself! It turned in a flash and crashed through the undergrowth and was gone.

Nosey jumped up and down with vexation, and in true Neanderthal fashion they all stood and shouted at each other, particularly at Dad, before they moved on to try again. Again Nosey's wonderful nose led the way, while Nosey muttered about lost opportunities, and they'd be dashed lucky to get another chance. But they did, almost straight away.

The trees were thinning out, there was very little cover, when Nosey said in a loud whisper, "Down, everybody!"

A small herd of deer was feeding and hadn't spotted the hunters, who dropped flat in the grass. Except one. Dad looked at the ground. It was damp and a bit muddy. One couldn't go around throwing oneself down on any old patch of ground, particularly wearing fully-fashioned fox fur robes. He knelt and began carefully to brush away some loose twigs and dead leaves. He covered the muddy bit with a handful of grass, then began gingerly to lower himself on to his stomach, taking care not to wrinkle his hunting robe. The hunters watched in total disbelief. And so did the deer . . . for a split second. Then they were gone, in a flash of white tails and a rattling of antlers on low branches.

There was absolutely no doubt whose fault it was this time, and Dad was made to go to the rear of the column, behind even the apprentices, where, it was decided, he could do the least harm.

And off trudged the hunting party once more.

"That's two chances we've missed," said

one. "I don't really suppose we'll get another."

"No," said another man. "It's only accidents that come in threes. But that's really two we've had already. What's going to happen next?"

"Oh, something really terrible, like an earthquake," said his friend, and they went on, braced for the next disaster. It came a few moments later.

Dad's voice came urgently from the tail of the column. "Listen! What's that?"

Behind them they could hear a thudding, rumbling noise accompanied by a crashing of undergrowth and getting closer every moment.

"An earthquake! I knew it!" cried someone.

Then, with a snort and a bellow, the "earthquake" was upon them. Bursting out of the trees came the most ferocious animal of the Ice Age world. Even the sabre-tooth tigers were afraid of the forest cattle, and it was the biggest imaginable forest bull which thundered down upon the Neanderthal hunters, the sharp tips of its great horns shining dangerously in the sunlight.

Someone shouted, "RUN!" which was a bit pointless, since the hunters were already scattering in all directions before the bull had caught more than its first glimpse of them. Before it had reached the centre of the clearing they were already safely in the branches of tall trees!

Except one!

While his companions sprinted for safety, their hunting robes flying wildly about them, Dad shambled as quickly as he could, hampered by the elegantly close-

fitting lines of his fully-fashioned red fox fur hunting robe. The bull whirled round, looking for its vanished victims, and saw Dad desperately trying to hitch up the robe as he ran. At the last moment he managed to sidestep the charging animal, and before it could turn for another charge he untied the strings which fastened the robe and pulled it off. Then he ran like the wind for the trees, the red fox robe over his arm. But, fast as he ran, the bull galloped faster. When the hoof beats were right behind him, Dad again side-stepped, and the bull passed so close that the wind almost knocked him off his feet.

From the safety of the trees, Littlenose and the hunters watched in astonishment as Dad ducked and dodged the bull. Every time Dad got close to a tree, the bull was somehow there first, ready to charge again.

After a particularly wild charge by the bull, Dad stood panting in the centre of the clearing, the red robe in one hand and trailing on the ground, and the bull glared with fierce red eyes from the edge of the forest, pawing at the ground and tossing its horns. Dad looked round for the nearest tree, and he had his back to the bull when it charged. He whirled at the last second, the robe flying out, and the bull raced past, skidded to a halt and came at him again. This happened several times, then Littlenose suddenly shouted, "It's the ROBE! It's not YOU it's after, Dad. It thinks the ROBE'S ALIVE! Drop the robe and save yourself!"

"Not likely!" shouted back Dad as he leapt yet again to safety. "This robe cost me twenty green pebbles. No bull's going to get it . . . no matter how big it is!" And he pirouetted quite gracefully with the robe flying over the bull's horns which missed Dad by a hair's breadth.

The hunters clung to their branches, astounded. It was really very exciting. Littlenose didn't know that Dad could be so agile, but then it wasn't every day that Dad had a giant forest bull after him with its long sharp horns. But Dad was beginning to tire. As the bull charged he just stood and swung the robe in a circle so that the bull skidded by under his outstretched arm, and Nosey leaned from his tree and shouted, "Olé!"

Dad looked up at the sound of Nosey's voice, and in that moment the bull caught the tip of one horn in the hem of the robe,

nearly pulling
Dad off his
feet before
it was torn
from his
grasp.
While the
bull knelt
on the fallen
robe and ripped
and slashed at it with
its horns, two of the hunters dashed across
the clearing and dragged Dad to the safety
of the trees.

The last sight any of them had of the
red fox fur hunting robe was a glimpse of a
tattered fragment flying from the tip of a
horn as the bull, with a triumphant snort,
disappeared into the depths of the forest.

That is, if you don't count the squidgy patch of trodden earth, mashed-up grass, leaves and fragments of red fur in the middle of the clearing.

"That was my fully-fashioned red fox fur hunting robe," wailed Dad, almost in tears. "I'll never have one like that again."

"Good," said Nosey, unsympathetically.

As they prepared to set off home, Littlenose said to Nosey, "Mr Nosey, what was that you shouted back there? When Dad dodged the bull? 'Olé!' or something."

"I don't really know," said Nosey. "It just seemed sort of appropriate."

And he set about sorting out the party into their correct order for the trek back to the caves.

Two-Eyes' Friends

Littlenose's best friend was Two-Eyes, his pet mammoth. Great herds of wild mammoths roamed the land. They usually kept clear of the places where people lived, but occasionally, if food was scarce, they would be seen close at hand, and Littlenose had several times watched from a safe distance as a herd went by.

The young mammoths were the same

size as Two-Eyes but the grown-up ones towered as tall as trees, with long powerful trunks and enormous curved tusks.

One day, Littlenose was playing one of his own very complicated games outside the cave where he lived. It involved twigs and stones and patterns in the sand, and was so intricate that only he really understood it. Two-Eyes, who was supposed to be playing, eventually gave up and wandered away by himself.

He made his way up the hill behind the cave and on to the grassy upland beyond. It was a lovely day, and a fresh wind was blowing.

Two-Eyes snuffed at the breeze with his trunk. It was full of all sorts of interesting smells. He took another snuffle, and his eyes grew round with excitement. His ears spread out and his trunk held straight in front of him, he trotted forward, following an unusual scent. It grew stronger every moment, until he came to the edge of a hollow, and saw something that made him squeal with delight.

It was a huge herd of mammoths!

The great males were standing on the edge of the crowd, keeping watch for any cave lion or sabre-toothed tiger who might fancy a piece of mammoth steak for lunch. The females gathered in groups exchanging mammoth gossip, while there were dozens of young ones, like Two-Eyes, running and jumping and playing all over the place.

Two-Eyes gave a little squeal and trotted down into the hollow. The young mammoths stopped playing and watched him suspiciously. One of them came over to Two-Eyes. They snuffled at each other and grunted and squeaked in mammoth talk, and a moment later were firm friends. The others crowded round, and they too squeaked and grunted at Two-Eyes, and soon it was as if they had known each other all their lives.

Then the games started again. They ran races, played tug-of-war with their trunks, and did a wonderful dance. Each held the tail of the one in front in his trunk, while they wound their way in a long snaky line through the hollow, much to the annoyance of the grown-ups.

Two-Eyes was enjoying himself so much that he forgot the time. Only when the sun was getting low in the sky did he realize that it was late, and that he ought to be thinking of going home.

He trumpeted "Good-bye" to his friends and started to leave. But they didn't want him to go! They came running after him, and crowded round, while Two-Eyes desperately tried to explain that he had to go.

They would come too, they squealed; and Two-Eyes couldn't make them understand that he lived in a cave with Littlenose and his mother and father. The mammoths didn't want to be parted from their new friend, and in the end, Two-Eyes set off with them all crowding round him.

Meanwhile, Littlenose had realized that Two-Eyes had not returned, and it was getting near bedtime. He stood at the cave entrance and called: "TWO-EYES!"

But there was no answer.

He called again, and was just about to set off to look for him in the woods when, looking up, he saw a black shape appear on the crest of the hill behind the cave. "Come on, Two-Eyes," he shouted. "It's late. Almost bedtime."

The black shape started running down the hill, and Littlenose was about to turn away when he gasped in horror. Not one, but dozens of little black mammoths were coming over the crest. Like a black, furry wave they poured over and down, heading straight for the cave. Littlenose turned to run . . . but he was too late.

The mammoths swept past and over him, knocking him off his feet. In a cloud of dust, and squealing and snorting, they rushed straight into the cave.

Pots broke, the supper was trampled underfoot, the fire was stamped out and Mum and Dad were pushed up flat against the back of the cave.

Mum was speechless . . . but Dad wasn't!

"LITTLENOSE!" he screamed. "Get them out! This is all your fault! Get these stupid creatures out before they knock the whole place down!"

Littlenose got safely behind a tree this time before he called: "TWO-EYES!"

Two-Eyes heard and came running out of the cave . . . but so did all the others. Once more the black furry tide swept around Littlenose, but this time it didn't knock him down.

"Please, Two-Eyes," said Littlenose. "I

don't know which one is you. Couldn't you please ask your friends to go home, and only you come when I call?

But of course the friends didn't want to go. They stood, pressed close around Littlenose, waiting to see what would happen next. They were enjoying this new game.

In the cave, Dad and Mum looked at the damage. It was dreadful. There was hardly a thing that hadn't been broken.

"That mammoth is the stupidest creature I know," said Dad, angrily.

"I'm sure he didn't mean it," said Mum, soothingly. "He was only playing with his friends. He's brought them visiting, and they want to meet us."

"Well," said Dad, "they won't get a second chance," and he began to block up the entrance with rocks, leaving only a space at one side.

"Come on, Littlenose," he called. "Hurry, or you'll be locked out."

"But I can't come without Two-Eyes," Littlenose wailed. "He can't stay out all night, and I don't know which is Two-Eyes. They all answer when I call."

"Two-Eyes should have thought of that
before he started all this foolishness,"
called back Dad. "Now hurry. It's getting
dark."

Littlenose was desperate. He just
couldn't leave Two-Eyes out all night, but
how was he to tell which one was his pet?

Then he remembered. Of course! How
silly could he get? Two-Eyes got his name

because his eyes were different colours – one red and one green. Other mammoths had two red eyes, all Littlenose had to do was look.

It took ages. The mammoths' long shaggy fur hung down over their eyes, and he had to go round each one, stroking it and carefully parting the fur over its eyes to see the colour. He had looked at more than half before he found Two-Eyes.

Dad was making impatient gestures from the cave, so Littlenose quickly leaned over and whispered in Two-Eyes' ear: "Do as I tell you, Two-Eyes, and go very slowly. We don't want this lot charging into the cave again. Now, come along."

Taking Two-Eyes' trunk in his hand, he led him slowly through the closely crowded mammoths. Those in front made way for

them, while those behind fell in to make a
sort of procession. Gradually, they drew
nearer to the cave. Littlenose let go of the
trunk, and began to steer Two-Eyes from
behind, aiming at the gap in the barricade.

Then, just as Two-Eyes's head was in the
cave, Littlenose gave him an enormous
push, while at the same time he whirled
round with a yell and waved his arms.

Two-Eyes scrambled into the cave, while the mammoths scattered in all directions. Littlenose jumped inside, and Dad quickly blocked the opening.

All night the little creatures cried and whimpered outside for their friend. Occasionally, a small trunk would poke through a chink in the rocks, and no one got a wink of sleep.

However, just before daybreak, they heard the most dreadful noise. There were loud trumpetings and crashings and the thunder of many great feet. Dad peeped out.

"It's the mammoths!" he cried. "They've come for their young."

The adults were very angry with the young ones for running away, and were slapping and spanking them with their trunks while chasing them home. The loud

noises went on for a long time, but
eventually died away in the distance.

In the morning, everything looked a bit
flattened, but otherwise there was no sign
of the mammoth herd.

Later in the day Littlenose climbed up
to the hollow. But the mammoths had gone
from there too, and although in the
following weeks Two-Eyes visited the
hollow hopefully, they never came back.